Fennings Taylor

The Hon. Thos. D'Arcy McGee

a sketch of his life and death

Fennings Taylor

The Hon. Thos. D'Arcy McGee
a sketch of his life and death

ISBN/EAN: 9783337095581

Printed in Europe, USA, Canada, Australia, Japan

Cover: Foto ©Raphael Reischuk / pixelio.de

More available books at **www.hansebooks.com**

THE

HON. THOS. D'ARCY McGEE:

A SKETCH

OF HIS

LIFE AND DEATH,

By FENNINGS TAYLOR,

DEPUTY CLERK AND CLERK ASSISTANT OF THE SENATE OF CANADA.
AUTHOR OF SKETCHES OF BRITISH AMERICANS,

WITH A

CABINET-SIZE PORTRAIT BY W. NOTMAN.

New Edition :--Revised and Enlarged.

MONTREAL:

PRINTED BY JOHN LOVELL, ST. NICHOLAS STREET.

1868.

THE HONORABLE THOMAS D'ARCY MCGEE

OF MONTREAL.

> Rob me of all the joys of sense,
> Curse me with all but impotence,
> Fling me upon an ocean oar,
> Cast me upon a savage shore;
> SLAY ME! but own above my bier
> " The man now gone still held while here
>   The jewel Independence ! "
>   CANADIAN BALLADS,
>   *By Thomas D'Arcy McGee*

HAD the Honorable Thomas D'Arcy McGee lived in the middle of the sixth century he would very probably have been a member, and a very distinguished one too, of that all-powerful " Bardic Order," before whose awful anger, Mr. McGee informs us in his History of Ireland, " kings trembled and warriors succumbed in superstitious dread." This influential order, we are elsewhere told, were " the editors, professors, registrars, and record keepers " of those early days ; the makers and masters of public opinion, whose number in the provinces of Meath and Ulster alone, in the reign of king Hugh the second, exceeded twelve hundred. Although the subject of our sketch was neither a prophet, nor the son of a prophet, it is not improbable that, could we trace his genealogy aright, we might discover that the trunk of his family tree is rooted and grounded in poetic earth ; for his intellectual life derived no slight nourishment from the poet's heritage,—imagination and fancy. Mr. McGee's ancestors hailed originally from Ulster. It is therefore probable he derived through them from the imposing commonwealth of bards to which we have referred, and that his scholar-like forefathers may be looked for among the twelve hundred whom king Hugh impeached, but who were upheld and defended by the magnanimous St. Columbcille, who, moved by a love of letters, a schoolman's sympathies, and a christian man's duties, expressly journeyed from his sea-girt home at Icolumkill to appear as counsel for his brethren at the rude tribunal of the irascible king.   On referring to one of the larger and more perfect maps of Ireland, and looking closely along the north-eastern coast, we shall perceive situated sea-ward off the shore of Antrim, in the province of Ulster, and within the ancient barony of Belfast, a small islet which bears the name of " Island Magee."   This little sea-washed speck contained, according to one of the latest, if not the latest topographical survey, about seven thousand acres of the finest land in the northern part of the kingdom.   Moreover, in 1837 it was peopled by no less than two thousand six hundred and ten inhabitants.   In the early times, the lordship of the Island was vested in the great Ulster family of O'Neil, from whom it passed in the sixteenth century to the Macdonalds of the Antrim Glens, and in the seventeenth, by the fortune of arms, to the Chichesters, Earls of Belfast and Marquises of Donegal.   From this small Island, for which the original tenants are said to have paid the annual rental of " two goshawks and a pair of gloves," (which, by the way, may have been considered enough, since, to an incredibly recent period, the Island was imagined by its inhabitants to be a theatre of sorcery,)—their descendants were almost exterminated, and wholly expelled by a force of covenanters at the time when the memorable Munroe was commander of the Parliamentary armies in Ireland.   Three only of those who bore the name of Magee were said to have escaped to the mainland, and from one of those three, who we suspect must have appropriated more than his share of the sorcery, the subject of our sketch accounted himself to have directly descended.

Without dwelling further on the facts and incidents of his remote ancestry, we may mention that the Honorable Thomas D'Arcy McGee is the second son of the late Mr. James McGee, of Wexford, and of Dorcas Morgan, his wife.   He was born at Carlingford, in the County of Louth, on the 13th of April, 1825, a day which has since then become a day of mourning in his family.   The name of

"D'Arcy," by which Mr. McGee was conventionally known, is, we have understood, derived from his god-father Mr. Thomas D'Arcy, a gentlemen who resided in the neighborhood of Carlingford, and, as we may infer, a personal friend of the family. Of his parents Mr. McGee was accustomed to speak with filial affection and becoming reverence, for he was early taught to "honor his father and his mother." But for the memory of the latter, whom he lost at a very early age, he entertained feelings of tender and enthusiastic admiration. Such feelings appear to be almost divinely wrought, and, like threads of gold, they beautify as well as strengthen the purest fibres of our nature. On the mind of Mr. McGee they exerted the gentle influence of poetry as well as the holy one of love. Separate qualities, such as duty and respect, obedience and devotion, love and pride, when looked at through the lens of his memory, cease to be distinct. All his recollections of his mother, though differently colored, nevertheless met and blended harmoniously in his character, not unlike the soft hues of the rainbow, as in the hush of evening they silently melt in a sea of light.

No doubt there were strong intellectual affinities between the mother and her son ; and this sympathetic attraction created an indelible impression on the heart of the latter. The intellectual charts of the two minds were, we are inclined to think, marked with not dissimilar lines ; bold and deeply drawn in the case of the son, they were sketchily traced and delicately shaded in the instance of the mother. The subtle charm of divine poesy seems to have pervaded both; and this spell of fancy and feeling, of imagination and truth, may, in some sort, account for the magnetic attractions which governed the intercourse of the parent and child.

To talk about his mother was, as all who know him had occasion to observe, a source of unalloyed happiness to her son. As in a holiday in his boyhood, so the acids of controversy and the sharp edges of strife gave place to expressions tipped with sunshine, when his lips could be beguiled into speaking of what his heart never ceased to feel.

> "My mother ! at that holy name
> Within my bosom there's a gush
> Of feeling, which no time can tame,
> A feeling which for years of fame
> I would not, could not crush ! "

According to his recollection of her, the subject of our sketch
was accustomed to allude to his mother as a person of genius and
acquirements, rare in her own or in any other class. She was
endowed, as Mr. McGee commonly observed, with a fertile imagination and a cultivated mind. Moreover nature had given her
a sweet voice and an exquisite ear, and the latter prescribed ·exact
laws to the former when, bird-like, she thought fit to attune that
voice to song. She was fond of music, as well as of its twin
sister, poetry. A diligent reader of the best books, she was also
an intelligent lover of the best ballads. She liked especially those
of Scotland. The poetry of common life was in her case no mere
figure of speech. Through all the changes of daily duty there ran
a vein of fancy, which enabled her to brighten the real with the
pleasant phantasies of the ideal, and support the dark cares of the
mind on the white wings of the imagination. McNeil's words

> " Oh whar hae you been a' the day
>   My boy Tammie ! "

were the words with which she usually greeted and welcomed her
favorite child. In common with her contemporaries, the mothers
of her day, she appears to have had a special liking for Home's
tragedy of Douglas ; and we may perhaps more easily imagine than
describe her sense of pride as she listened to " Tammie's" earliest
lesson in elocution. It is not difficult to see the curly-headed urchin
standing on a table, and in melo-dramatic guise, with precocious
effrontery informing his mother, who knew better, and his mother's
friends who did not believe him, that

> " My name is Norval."

His mother, as we have said, was early removed from him by death.
We will not speak of, since we cannot describe, grief. We may,
however, conjecture, since their natures and intellectual tastes were
identical, that her death was like a severance of himself from himself.
The tears, for he was not ashamed to weep, which no doubt
fell upon her grave, were neither idle nor unavailing tears, for
they became as it were so many cameras through which were
reflected the duties, the incidents, and the obligations of his

future life. Thus at the age of seventeen we find D'Arcy McGee had passed the shallows where timid youths bathe and shiver, and had boldly struck out into the deep sea of duty. We have no data which will enable us to bridge the time between his mother's death and his arrival on this continent: but it is not difficult to suppose that it was filled up in the manner usual to youth, with the difference only of a greater amount of application and a higher range of study. On arriving at Boston, he became almost immediately connected with the press of that city. Kind fortune seemed to befriend him; for his lot appeared to be cast in, what was at that time, and perhaps still is, the intellectual capital of the United States—the forcing-house of its fanaticism, and the favored seat of its scholarship. Thus it was that D'Arcy McGee, a youth hungry and thirsty for knowledge, influence and fame, found himself a resident of the New England States capital, with access to the best public libraries on this side of the Atlantic, and within reach of the best public lecturers on literary and scientific subjects. For at that day Emerson, Giles, his county and country-man, Whipple, Chapin, and Brownson, lived in that city or in its vicinity. It was moreover the residence of Channing, Bancroft, Eastburn, Prescott, Ticknor, Longfellow, Lowell, Holmes, and others, whose works should have purified the moral atmosphere, and have made Boston to others, what we suppose it must have been to them, an appreciative and congenial home. It is not difficult to imagine, from what we knew and could observe of his mature man-hood, that D'Arcy McGee, the impulsive Irish lad, overflowing with exuberant good nature and untiring industry, with his heart full of hope and his brain full of ambition, soon found his way into meetings where learned men delivered lectures, or among the book-sellers, whose shops such celebrities frequented. Neither is it a matter for surprise that he early attracted the notice of several of their number. Opportunities of speaking publicly are by no means uncommon in the United States, and we should imagine that Boston contained a great many nurseries, under different names, where the alphabet of the art could be acquired. Whether the scholar progresses beyond his letters depends very much on the furnishing of his mind. The nerve and knack may be got by practice, but the prime condition,—having something to say,—must spring from

exact thought and severe study. We have every reason to believe
that even in his early youth, the subject of our sketch, observed
that condition; but we have no means of knowing where or in what
way he acquired the fluent habit of graceful and polished oratory.
For since he was enthroned on his mother's tea-table, and declared
to listening friends that his name was "Norval," we have been
unable to discover any intermediate audience between his select
one at Carlingford, and his scientific one at Boston. Strange as
it may seem, it is we believe, no less true than strange, that
during his sojourn at Boston, from the years 1842 to 1845, when
between the ages of seventeen and twenty, he had actually made
his mark as a public speaker. Nor was it denied, that the audacious youth, though contemptuously styled "Greenhorn," and
"Paddy-boy," very fairly held his own with men who never were
"green" and who had long ceased to be "boys." It may be
observed in passing that the "Know-nothing" party, which has
since then acquired consistency and influence, in its incipient shape,
was discernible at that day under the name of the Anti-foreign
party, a party which Mr. McGee could not do otherwise than
criticise with severity and oppose with vehemence.

At the period we refer to, the "Lyceum System" as it has been
termed, spread itself over the New England States. People desired
to receive knowledge distilled through the brains of their neighbors. Lecturers were at a premium; and youth forestalled time by
discoursing of wisdom, irrespective of experience. Thus it was that
D'Arcy McGee, with a boy's down on his chin, and with whiskers
in embryo, itinerated among our neighbors, and gave them the
advantage of listening to a youthful lecturer, discoursing, we must
be permitted to think, on aged subjects. What those subjects were
may be partially conjectured, for the reminiscences of his lecturing
life in those days were full of amusing as well as of instructive
incident; more especially as the period was, we think, coeval with
a transition phase not only of the Irish, but of the American, mind.

Mixing, as he necessarily must have done, with all sorts and con-
ditions of men, it was impossible that Mr. McGee should not have
formed many acquaintances of more or less valuable, and some friend-
ships, perhaps, beyond price. Among the latter it was his practice
to make grateful mention of Mr. Grattan, then Her Majesty's

Consul at Boston. Besides a name historically eloquent which he inherited, that gentlemen, unquestionably possessed great intellectual acquirements as well as personal gifts. In the latter were included a kindly disposition and a cordial manner. It was therefore natural enough that he should have taken a warm interest in his enthusiastic countryman, and from the treasury of his own experience have given the young writer and lecturer many valuable hints on the style and structure of literary work. Thus it chanced that the wise counsellor and the kind friend meeting in the same person, exerted no inconsiderable influence on the young enthusiast. Mr. Grattan's sympathies fell upon an appreciative mind, and were destined at a later period of life to exert no inconsiderable influence on his character; for Mr. McGee always spoke of the Consul with admiration and of his services with gratitude.

A new page in his eventful life was however about to be opened. The obscure lad who had turned his back upon Ireland was about to be beckoned home again by the country he had left. The circumstances, apart from their political significance, were in the highest degree complimentary to one who at the time was not " out of his teens." An article, written by Mr. McGee, on an Irish subject, in a Boston newspaper, having attracted the attention of the late Mr. O'Connell, the former received, early in the year 1845, a very handsome offer from the proprietors of the *Freeman's Journal*, a Dublin daily paper, for his editorial services. This proposal he accepted, and hence his personal participation in the Irish politics of the eventful years which commenced then and ended in 1848. Ardent by temperament, and enthusiastic by disposition, it was almost impossible for him to keep within the bounds of moral force which Mr. O'Connell had prescribed, and which the newspaper he served was instructed to advocate. Mr. McGee felt that such fetters galled him, and he became impatient under their restraint. The habit of maintaining his own convictions was a necessity of his condition. Controlled by his imagination and following the lead of his feelings, he determined at all hazards to associate himself with the more advanced and enthusiastic section of the liberal party, then known by the name of " Young Ireland." This section or *coterie*, for it was scarcely a party, possessed many attractions for such an adherent. Besides the name, and the bright, alluring, misleading quality of youth, which that name symbolized and expressed, the *coterie* was made up of those many-hued forms of intellectual mosaic work which men generally admire and rarely trust; very charming in our sight and very perishable in our service. It was composed, at least at first, almost altogether of young barristers, young doctors, young college men and young journalists, most of them under thirty, and many under twenty-five years of age. Mr. McGee was probably their most youthful member, for when his association with them commenced he was not of age. Of such hot blood was the " Young Ireland " party compounded, that little surprise was occasioned, and none was expressed, when its mischievous revels were broken up by the riot act. We cannot in a paper of this kind discuss the question at any length, but if we understand the history of those times aright, the policy of moral force which had guided O'Connell was not, in the first instance, discarded by his younger and more ardent disciples. They wished to accomplish the purpose of " The Liberator," only they desired to shorten the time and accelerate the speed of the operation. They thought that O'Connell was " old and slow." They felt that they were young and active. In their minds the rivalry between age and youth was renewed, provoking the old issues and re-enacting the old results. Keeping in view the great end which they had set themselves to accomplish, they nevertheless sought, in the first instance, to move by literary rather than by political appliances. Accordingly they planned, among other works, a series of stirring shilling volumes for the people, entitled the " Library of Ireland." The famine of 1847 extinguished the enterprize, but not until twenty volumes of this new National Library had been published. Of the above number Mr. McGee was the author of two. One, a series of biographies of illustrious Irishmen of the seventeenth century, and the other a memoir of Art. McMurrough, a half forgotten Irish king of the fourteenth century. Of course, works published under such circumstances, and forming parts of such a series, would at first, at all events, be well received and widely circulated. They were passionately written and greedly devoured by a people who were emaciated by famine and made desperate by pestilence. Still their merits could not have been of a mere evanescent character, for we are credibly informed that now, after a period of twenty years, the books retain much of their early popularity.

Mr. McGee, if we remember aright, has somewhere said, with respect to the transactions of those times, that "Young Ireland," not content to restore the past, endeavored to re-enact it; not content to write history, tried, to use a familiar phrase of Mr. John Sandfield Macdonald's, to "make it;" and we have little doubt, could we see the intellectual machinery which preceded those events, we should discover that none more than Mr. McGee assiduously labored to manufacture history.

The *coterie* grew into a confederation of which Mr. McGee was, we believe, the chief promoter and the chosen secretary. It was not without adherents, neither was it without attraction, and especially to the class, a by no means inconsiderable one, whose judgment is controlled by their imagination, and who seem to think that feeling and wisdom are identical qualities. We decline to indicate those transactions by any particular name. We all know that they were failures, and since time tempers judgment, we venture to believe that the chief actors of that day concur with the critics of the present time in thinking that they were follies. The most stirring among the many impassioned *Songs of the Nation,*—"Who fears to speak of '98"—showed alike the genius, the courage, and the credulity of "Young Ireland" of '48. The Irish politics of fifty years since were no more worthy of recall than was the Irish policy of two hundred years since. Young Ireland should not, we venture to think, have invoked the embarrasing memories of the past, if it wished to make old Ireland new. It was an error in time, an error in judgment, and an error in sense, which, fortunately for all, contained within itself the germ of inevitable failure.

While England, through her press and in her Parliament, scouted the policy and punished its principal exponents, she did not fail very generously to acknowledge the unquestionable talent and out-spoken honesty of that earnest and ill-fated party. We all know what followed. Some of the leaders were sent into penal exile, while others, including the subject of our sketch, found safety in voluntary expatriation. But the exploit was not unattended with excitement and peril, as the following narrative will more clearly show :—

After the secession of the Young Ireland party from Conciliation Hall, in 1846, under the leadership of the late Mr. Smith O'Brien, the confederation was established, and at all its meetings McGee was one of the most forcible and prominent speakers. He was not a favorite with many of the leading spirits of the party with whom he was associated; but he and Charles Gavan Duffy, who has since so conspicuously figured as a statesman in Australia, were always the fastest friends, and carried on with each other a friendly correspondence up to the time of his death. When the British Government suspended the *Habeas Corpus* Act in 1848, it was resolved at a meeting of the Executive Council, held at their rooms in D'Olier street, that this act of despotism should be resisted by force of arms, and for that purpose an appeal should be made to the country, and the prominent leaders sent into those districts where their influence with the peasantry was greatest. According to this arrangement, the late Smith O'Brien, the late Col. Doheny, and the late John B. Dillon, General Meagher, Richard O'Gorman, and others, left Dublin and proceeded to their assigned localities; but McGee was charged with bringing over from Glasgow an expedition which had been organized and armed in that city.— Descriptions of the leaders were published in the *Hue and Cry*—a sort of private police gazette—and rewards offered for their apprehension. The country was swarming with detectives; the railway depots were closely watched, and the stage coach lines placed under strict police scrutiny. The proclamation of the suspension of the *Habeas Corpus* Act was made in Dublin on a Sunday morning in July, 1848, but Mr. McGee departed suddenly from the city on Saturday evening, and arrived in Londonderry on the following morning, where he met a friend, as he was taking his matutinal walk upon the historic walls of the maiden city. The meeting occurred on a much-frequented spot of this very public promenade—it was exactly over Bishop's gate—McGee placed his finger on his lip, which his friend at once understood; no name was mentioned and they walked past Walker's monument out of Butcher's gate, through the suburb of Derry called the "bog side," into the country, and up the green hills which look upon the fair Lough Swilly, where Wolfe Tone was captured, upon the mountain of Gray Innishowea,

> "Where coward or traitor there never was none."

Mr. McGee briefly explained the proceedings of the previous forty-eight hours, the plan of action, and the duty to which he was detailed. The assizes which were about to commence the next day in Derry, brought many professional men from Dublin to the city, and it was therefore deemed prudent not to return to his hotel, where he stayed under the name of Doyle, until night had cast her shadows athwart the waters of the Foyle. The evening was spent in McGee's bed-room, where future prospects of success were enthusiastically discussed. His companion wrote a letter to his wife in Dublin, simply stating that Mr. Doyle had passed through Derry and was in good health and spirits. He was then scant of money, but expected to find a draft on his arrival in Glasgow, for which place he left by steamer the next evening. When he arived in Glasgow he met his friends, and put up at a hotel to await some intelligence of Smith O'Brien's movements. When he had been there a fortnight, he was discovered, and a warrant was being made out for his arrest, when intelligence reached the ears of a wealthy citizen, and a prominent member in the Repeal Association. That gentleman hastened to inform Mr. McGee of his danger, supplied him with the funds, and with him took the next train for Newcastle on-Tyne. When within a few miles of that place, they returned towards Glasgow, got out at a way station, and took the stage coach for a little port on the Scotch coast whence a steamer plies daily to Belfast, and makes the trip in about three hours and a half. This was lucky, for the police had hired a special train, passed them on the way, and were waiting for Mr. McGee at the Newcastle station. There was another passenger in the coach, but to his great horror that passenger was no other than the renowned Rev. Tresham Gregg, who was the great champion of the Orange and Government party in Ireland. Mr. McGee thought he would be delivered over by the reverend loyalist to the first policeman they should meet. But he was agreeably dissappointed; Tresham did not take the slightest notice of him, and soon himself and his carpet-bag were stowed away in the steamboat. He arrived in Belfast about midnight, walked to the station of the Ulster railway, took the train for Armagh, which he reached about daylight. From Armagh he proceeded to Omagh, in the county Tyrone, by jaunting car, thence to Enniskillen, and from that to Sligo, where the Ribbon men took charge of him, and concealed him for a fortnight at the base of the Benbulben Mountain. Here he remained in perfect security until he communicated with his friends in Glasgow, and funds were forwarded to him to enable him to escape from the country. His object was to reach Donegal or Derry, and get away by some ship leaving either of those ports for America. He moved from Benbulben, first to Donegal, and was concealed in the town and in the very house where Sir Thomas Blake, of Menio Castle, County Galway, was then stationed as one of Her Majesty's "Resident Magistrates." He remained there a week, and Sir Thomas got information of the fact on the very day he took his departure. The worthy Baronet gave close pursuit, and traced him up to Derry, where the late Bishop McGinn and some of his clergy rendered him effectual aid. He was provided with a clerical suit of clothes and a breviary. In the garb of a Catholic priest he was passed through the enemy's lines and put on board a ship anchored off Moville at the mouth of the Foyle, called the "Shamrock'" and commanded by Capt. John Moore, of Galway. He was several days at sea before he let the Captain know his real character, but his confidence was not misplaced. The captain treated him hospitably, and brought him safely to New York.

Thus it was that, heated and excited by the strife, angered and disappointed at the issue, Mr. McGee for a second time landed in the United States. As before, his occupations were those of a journalist and a lecturer, for it was his pleasure as well as his duty to live by the sweat of his brain. Between the close of 1848 and the commencement of 1857, he published two newspapers, *The New York Nation*, and the *American Celt*. It was, of course, natural, all the circumstances considered, that the inclination of his mind should have been violently, and from the force of recent experience and actual discipline, bitterly hostile to the government of Great Britain. Many will remember, not from the papers themselves, for they had but a small circulation in the Provinces, but from extracts which found a place in several of the Canadian journals, how fiercely and fanatically anti-English his political writings were. But while admitting the exaggerated rancour which characterized his words, it will undoubtedly be allowed that time and the opportunity for closer observation produced their usual influence on his instructed mind. His fierce anger towards Great Britain gradually disappeared. His excited temper, like the evil spirit of the son of Kish, was exorcised, if not by the spell of music, at least by the taming influence of time, the force of acquired truth and the sense of obvious wrong. The book of remembrance and the book of experience were before him. He could read their letter-press and criticise their illustrations. He could see his country-men under British and his countrymen under American rule. He could look from that picture to this, from monarchical England to republican America, and with all the imperfections of the former, he might and probably did express his judgment of the contrast in the words of the Prince of Denmark, that taken all in all "it was Hyperion to a Satyr."

We could not, even in the cursory sketch which our limited space will permit us to make, pass over in silence Mr. McGee's personal and political career previous to his residence in Canada, for a por-tion of that career was a prelude to, and directly connected with, its more recent sequences amongst ourselves. His occupations during that period were professedly those of an author and a lecturer, and only accidentally those of a politician. Those occupations were marked with many errors and crossed with many vicissitudes. Still it must be allowed that if one of his ardent temperament and peculiar position succeeded in avoiding misfortune, he could hardly be expected to escape mistakes. An Irishman by birth, a Roman Catholic by parentage, passionately attached to his race, and devoutly loyal to his religion, he was from the very outset of his career remarkable for the courageous spirit of independence with which he formed and maintained his opinions, no matter whether the subjects on which he adventured them were political, historical, or social. One of his Canadian ballads illustrates this phase of his character, and supplies a key-note to his conduct: The last stanza which prefaces this sketch will be read with mourn-ful interest for it seems to have been laden with the crimson burden of foreknowledge. The first is as follows :

> " Let fortune frown and foes increase,
> And life's long battle know no peace,
> Give me to wear upon my breast
> The object of my early quest,
> Undimm'd, unbroken, and unchang'd,
> The talisman I sought and gain'd,
>   The jewel, Independence !"

Neither was it a mere poetical profession of faith. Mr. McGee's history very clearly shows that he had reason for his rhyme. In the very dew of his youth he maintained his political principles against such an opponent as the great O'Connell, and later still he wore his " Jewel Independence" in the presence of the late Dr. Hughes, the distinguished Archbishop of New York. It is probable that neither of those eminent men viewed with complacency what must have appeared like presumption on the part of their youthful antagonist, and the latter especially may have detected in the attitude thus assumed a certain amount of spiritual independence which that Prelate regarded as perilous to his religious welfare ; but it is pleasant to believe, as we have some reason to believe, that with manly generosity, those gifted gentlemen did not fail to express their respect for Mr. McGee's abilities, their appreciation of his sincerity, and their desire for his success in life.

The independence which Mr. McGee valued and apostrophized was not the independence which he found in the United States. His second sojourn in that country thoroughly disenchanted him. His early admiration paled before his later experience. The homœopathic principle appears to be susceptible of political as well as physical application, for a taste of democratic institutions cured Mr. McGee, as it has cured many besides him, of any tendency to democracy. Neither was social life in America more attractive than political life. Both were an offence, and one was an abomination. But the double discovery was made only after a painful and protracted effort not to see it, for it was with great reluctance that his vigorous mind and tenacious will surrendered their preconceived impressions and yielded at length to the irrefragable force of such unwelcome truths. It would be interesting to read, perchance we may have the opportunity of reading, Mr. McGee's own account of his rise and progress towards higher moral and physical latitudes, for every inch of his course might point a moral, every stage of his journey adorn a tale. They only who know with what fanatic faith the human mind will cling even to a cheat, can appreciate the wrench which follows the discovery of the cheat. No man can deliberately break his idol without some sorrowful remembrance of the thing he once thought divine. The testimony of Mr. McGee might enable us to compare the attractions

of his fancy with the fallacies of his experience,—the dream-land
which his imagination painted and the real land which his eyes saw.

In this interval of conflict, while fighting against himself, and by
wager of battle as it were, testing the strength and quality of his principles and opinions, new light, and with it new views, from an un-
looked-for quarter, seemed to cross his path.   In the midst of literary work in New York he made the acquaintance of many friends
in Canada.   Having formed his own opinions of the people whom
he had met, it was natural enough he should wish to see the country where they dwelt.   Thus it was that Mr. McGee, during one
summer vacation, taking a holiday after the manner of an editor,
found himself writing letters to his paper from the shores of Lake
Huron, at another from the solitudes of the Ottawa, and at a third
from the scenic Provinces of New Brunswick and Nova Scotia.   The
Provincial attractions were too much for him.   He heard in the
Provinces what he did not hear in the States, honest opinions openly expressed.   He found in the Provinces what he failed to find in
the States, a tangible security for freedom.   The promise of liberty
was no spurious or counterfeit debenture.   It was impressed with
the stamp of law and endorsed with the sign-manual of authority.
Whatever may have been the form of the fascination, we find that
in the early part of the year 1857, after, as we have the right to
suppose, a careful comparison of the two states of society, the
American and the Canadian, Mr. McGee transferred, as he has
somewhere said, " his household goods to the valley of the St. Lawrence," selecting the City of Montreal as the place of his abode.
We may here add that the City of Montreal lost no time in return-
ing the compliment, for on the first opportunity that city elected him
as one of its representatives in Parliament, and a little later his friends
and neighbors presented him with an exceedingly well-appointed
homestead in one of its most eligible localities.   It was a hearty
Irish mode of making him welcome.   Mr. McGee very modestly
sought only to be a citizen of the country ; his friends determined
that he should be a freeman.   No doubt the gift represented a great
honor of no uncertain value to the object of it.   But apart from such
considerations, the shape which the testimonial took, soothed and
flattered Irish sentiment, for if there be one form of property dearer
than another to the offspring of Erin, it is that of a holding ; and no

matter whether it be a park or a potato patch, it is equally precious if it promotes the possessor to the condition of an estated gentleman or a landed proprietor.

The old vocation was revived in Mr. McGee's new home. To write, to print, to publish were with him not only habits of life, but modes of enjoyment.

> "The long, long weary day
> Would pass in grief away,"

at least to him, if it uttered no speech from his pen, or received no thought from his brain. The time which elapsed between his arrival at Montreal, and the isssue of the first number of his news- ' paper, the *New Era*, was brief enough ; but it was nevertheless of sufficient length to enable him to sketch through its columns a policy which harmonized with the name of his paper. He earnestly advocated, and continued to advocate to the last hour of his life, an early union of all the colonies of British North America. In doing so, we may observe in passing, he initiated a phrase descriptive of his object, a phrase which has since become familiar alike from use and criticism, for the proposed confedcracy in his mind and writings was felicitously associated with the idea of a " new nationality."

At the general election in 1858, Mr. McGee's public career in — Canada commenced. He was returned to Parliament as one of the three representatives of Montreal. Whether from hereditary habit, a playful disposition, or serious thought, we know not, but on his arrival in the Province, he lost no time in declaring himself in true Hibernian style to be " against the government." And against the government he undoubtedly was during the four years of the continuance of irritating and acrimonious sixth Parliament. Much of course was expected of him. He had a certain repute as a politician, though he was more distinctly known as a forcible writer, and a fluent speaker. Still, his earlier Parliamentary efforts were, we think, followed by disappointment to those who had thought him to be capable of better and wiser things. It was observed that he was a relentless quiz, an adroit master of satire, and the most active of partizan sharpshooters. Many severe, some ridiculous, and not a few savage things were said by him. Thus from his affluent treasury of caustic and bitter irony he contributed not a little to the personal and Parliamentary embarrassments of those times. Many of the speeches of that period we would rather forget than remember. Some were not complimentary to the body to which they were addressed, and some of them were not creditable to the persons by whom they were delivered. It is true that such speeches secured crowded galleries, for they were sure to be either breezy or ticklish, gusty with rage, or grinning with jests. They were therefore the raw materials out of which mirth is manufactured, and consequently they ruffled tempers that were remarkable for placidity, and provoked irrepressible laughter in men who were regarded as too grave to be jocose. Of course they were little calculated to elicit truth, or promote order, or attract respect to the speaker. Indeed men who were inclined to despondency affected little reserve in saying that Parliamentary government was in their opinion a failure. During his early career, Mr. McGee appeared chiefly to occupy himself in saying unpleasant and severe things; in irritating the smoothest natures, and brushing every body's hair the wrong way. This occupation was apt to include the habit of making personal allusions the reverse of agreeable, and, as a matter of course, creating personal enmities the reverse of desirable. In truth, Mr. McGee's speeches at that time were garnished with so many merry jests, and sometimes overlaid with so much rancorous levity, that their more valuable parts were hidden from ordinary eyes, and inappreciable to ordinary minds. The cookery was too generous, the condiments were too spicy. The sauce bore to the substance about the same proportional inequality that Falstaff's " sack " did to his bread ; and this deficiency of solidity was attributed by many people to an absence of intellectual property, rather than to an error of conventional taste. Hence arose a disposition on the part of some to underrate Mr. McGee's mental strength, and hence, too, the observation, which, however, was more remarkable for glibness than accuracy, that "Mr. McGee speaks better than he reasons." Certainly the Parliamentary skirmishes of that period, though difficult to defend, were delightful to witness. Human drollery made up in some sort for human naughtiness. There were, for example, two members of that house of great ability, but very dissimilar habits of thought. They sat not far from one another, for if at that day they were not exactly " friends in council," they usually voted together. One was the present Attorney General West, the unrivalled chief of Parliamentary debate ; and the other, the present learned member for Brome, the intellectual detective of suspected fallacies. Breadth and subtlety, reason and casuistry, extensive observation and minute knowledge, marked then as now the peculiar characters of their modes of thought. No matter, however, whether the range of their reasoning was broad or deep, horizontal or vertical, circular or lateral, profound or peculiar, it was commonly acknowledged by the subject of our sketch in a cheerful Irish way, amusing enough to the spectator, but probably not as agreeable to those who looked for grave reflections on grave thoughts. The truth is, that Mr. McGee always seemed to be, in spite of himself, either mischievous or playful ; and regardless alike of the place or the occasion, he appeared to be seized with an irresistible impulse to splash every body with his paddle, and thus scatter about him an uncomfortable kind of melo-dramatic spray, which occasionally drifted and thickened into a rain of searching, infectious, comic banter, and which, as a matter of course, amidst roars of laughter, would drown reason, logic and speech in a flood of exuberant fun. Such efforts, however, did not always succeed. Indeed, more clever than praiseworthy, they scarcely deserved success, for people do not always admire what they laugh at. Reaction follows every kind of excess. Members began to talk of decorum of debate, and the necessity of recalling the House to a state of order. None better than Mr. McGee knew that he could, if occasion needed, be grave as well as gay, wise as well as witty, serious as well as jocose. He knew that he could lead thought as well as provoke mirth. He knew that at the fitting time he could make for himself a name, and for his adopted country a place, which would attract respect and honor in both hemispheres.

Having fairly looked his work in the face, Mr. McGee very naturally as we conjecture, cast about him for fitting co-operators. This portion of his public life seems to have been beset with perplexing peculiarities, as his party associations seem to have been the result of the merest accident. With an upper-crust of paradox there must, we may suppose, have been an undercurrent of contradiction. To be sure he chose his side, but in the presence of his declared principles and published opinions it is difficult to understand by what laws his choice was determined. On his arrival in Canada, he had, for reasons which he deemed to be sufficient, declared himself to be "against the government." Nor can it be denied that for the space of six years he proved the sincerity of his declaration. On the 20th May, 1862, the fortress which he had so persistently battered, fell, for the Cartier-Macdonald administration, which he had opposed and denounced, having been defeated on the motion for reading the Militia Bill the second time, was constrained to resign. In the Sandfield Macdonald-Sicotte administration, which succeeded to power, the subject of our sketch was offered and accepted the office of President of the Council. On the 8th of May following, on a question of want of confidence, the last mentioned administration found itself to be in a minority of five. Four days afterwards Parliament was prorogued with a view to its immediate dissolution. After the prorogation, Mr. Sandfield Macdonald, the leader of the Government, undertook the responsibility of directing what was equivalent to the very hazardous military manœuvre of changing his front in the presence of an active and sagacious enemy. No doubt he was obliged to strengthen his position, and under any circumstances his mode of doing so would be subject to criticism. He reconstructed his government, and the operation included, amongst other changes, not only the sending of his Irish forces to the rear, but of reducing them to the ranks, with the option, as it was amusingly made to appear, of being mustered out of the service. The transaction is of recent occurrence, and need not be dwelt upon. The surprise which it occasioned remains; for no very specific reasons have been given, so far as we are aware, for the course which was then pursued. That it was not taken upon the advice of the subject of our sketch, we have the best reason for thinking ; for Mr. McGee took the earliest opportunity of showing, in the general election which followed, that he would not play pawn to Mr. Sandfield Macdonald's king. Rather than do so he crossed over to the enemy. The amenities of political elections is a work yet to be written; when it is written, the election for Montreal, in 1863, might, we incline to think, furnish some instructive as well as amusing passages. In the session which immediately followed, Mr. McGee, on three different occasions, and with evident and unalloyed satisfaction, recorded his vote of want of confidence in the re-constructed administration of his former chief. Thus had he fairly crossed the House. He not only, and with a will, voted with the party which he had theretofore opposed, but in the month of March following, on the late Sir E. P. Taché being called upon to form an administration, and a strong party administration too, he accepted the office of Minister of Agriculture, which he continued to fill to the 1st July, 1867. People may be inclined to think, and not without some reason, that the subject of our sketch was moved in the course which he took more by pique than by principle, and that a personal slight provoked his political defection. Without staying to discuss a question on which we are not informed, we may, perhaps, be permitted to ask another, which to us, at least, appears to be still more perplexing. What were the circumstances which in the first instance separated Mr. McGee from the party of which he continued to be a conspicuous member to the day of his death? Were it not ill-mannered to pry, we might, perchance, amuse ourselves by indulging in some idle speculations, and supplement them by making some curious enquiries.

If there was one question more than another with which Mr. McGee had identified his name, that question was the union of all the Provinces, and as connected with, and inseparable from it, the questions of National defence, of the Inter-colonial Railway, and of Free Inter-colonial Trade. Happily these questions are not now the property of a party. They belong to the whole of British America, for they have been accepted by the great majority of its inhabitants, as well as by the government and the people of England. Still it should not be forgotten, that these great questions were parts of the cherished policy of the administration which Mr. McGee opposed, rather than of the administration to which he belonged. The law which regulates political relationships is not easily adjusted, for it is not unfrequently embarrassed with vexatious personal entanglements. In the instance before us, though we may see the affront which impelled, and suspect the causes which attracted him towards his present alliance, we do not see, nor are we required to see, why he served a seven year's apprenticeship to a a party whose policy, in many important particulars, was not only different from, but opposed to his own.

Passing from Mr. McGee's history as a party-man, to his opinions as a public one, we seem to emerge from a bewildering labyrinth of ill-lighted passages, into a succession of *salons* radiant with sunshine. We rise from what may be compared with the unseemly brawls of a parish vestry to the ennobling deliberations of a National Parliament. The vision of the "new era," which Mr. McGee, in his Montreal paper, foreshadowed in 1857, seems to have grown into shape and consistency. In an address delivered at the Temperance Hall, Halifax, in July, 1863, he thus sketched, and with a bold hand, the boundaries of British America, the Northern Empire of the future:

"A single glance at the physical geography of the whole of British America will show that it forms, quite as much in structure as in size, one of the most valuable sections of the globe. Along this eastern coast the Almighty pours the broad Gulf stream, nursed within the tropics, to temper the rigors of our air, to irrigate our 'deep sea pastures,' to combat and subdue the powerful Polar stream which would otherwise, in a single night, fill all our gulfs and harbors with a barrier of perpetual ice. Far towards the west, beyond the wonderful lakes, which excite the admiration of every traveller, the winds that lift the water-bearing clouds from the Gulf of Cortez, and waft them northward, are met by counter-currents which capsize them just where they are essential,—beyond Lake Superior, on both slopes of the Rocky Mountains. These are the limits of that climate which has been so much misrepresented, a climate which rejects every pestilence, which breeds no malaria, a climate under which the oldest stationary population—the French Canadian—have multiplied without the infusion of new blood from France or elsewhere, from a stock of 80,000 in 1760 to a people of 880,000 in 1860. I need not, however, have gone so far for an illustration of the fostering effects of our climate on the European race, when I look on the sons and daughters of this peninsula—natives of the soil for two, three, and four generations—when I see the lithe and manly forms on all sides, around and before me, when I see especially who they are that adorn that gallery (alluding to the ladies), the argument is over, the case is closed. If we descend from the climate to the soil, we find it sown by nature with these precious forests fitted to erect cities, to build fleets and to warm the hearts of many generations. We have the isothern of wheat on the Red River, on the Ottawa, and on the St. John; root crops everywhere; coal in Cape Breton and on the Saskatchewan; iron with us from the St. Maurice to the Trent; in Canada the copper-bearing rocks at frequent intervals from Huron to Gaspé; gold in Columbia and Nova Scotia; salt again, and hides in the Red River region; fisheries inland and seaward unequalled. Such is a rough sketch, a rapid enumeration of the resources of this land of our children's inheritance. Now what needs it this country,—with a lake and river and seaward system sufficient to accommodate all its own, and all its neighbor's commerce,—what needs such a country for its future? It needs a population sufficient in number, in spirit, and in capacity to become its masters; and this population need, as all civilized men need, religious and civil liberty, unity, authority, free intercourse, commerce, security and law."

Again, in the same paper, Mr. McGee exhibited the materials whereof the new nationality shall be composed:

"I endeavor to contemplate it in the light of a future, possible, probable, and I hope to live to be able to to say positive, British American Nationality. For I repeat, in the terms of the questions I asked at first, what do we need to construct such a nationality. Territory, resources by sea and land, civil and religious freedom, these we have already. Four millions we already are: four millions culled from the races that, for a thousand years, have led the van of Christendom. When the sceptre of Christian civilization trembled in the enervate grasp of the Greek of the Lower Empire, then the Western tribes of Europe, fiery, hirsute, clamorous, but kindly, snatched at the falling prize, and placed themselves at the head of human affairs. We are the children of these fire-tried kingdom founders, of these ocean-discoverers of Western Europe. Analyse our aggregate population: we have more Saxons than Alfred had when he founded the English realm. We have more Celts than Brien had when he put his heel on the neck of Odin. We have more Normans than William had when he marshalled his invading host along the strand of Falaise. We have the laws of St. Edward and St. Louis, Magna Charta and the Roman Code. We speak the speeches of Shakespeare and Bossuet. We copy the constitution which Burke and Somers and Sidney and Sir Thomas Moore lived, or died, to secure or save. Out of these august elements, in the name of the future generations who shall inhabit all the vast regions we now call ours, I invoke the fortunate genius of an United British America, to solemnize law with the moral sanction of religion, and to crown the fair pillar of our freedom with its only appropriate capital, lawful authority, so that hand in hand we and our descendants may advance steadily to the accomplishment of a common destiny."

And at St. John, New Brunswick, in the following month of the same year, Mr. McGee said: "There are before the public men of British America, at this moment, but two courses; either to drift with the tide of democracy, or to seize the golden moment and fix for ever the monarchical character of our institutions!" "I invite," he continues, "every fellow colonist who agrees with me to unite our efforts that we may give our Province the aspect of an Empire, in order to exercise the influence abroad and at home to create a State, and to originate a history which the world will not willingly let die!"

In another part of the same paper, Mr. McGee very solemnly said:

"This being my general view of my own duty—my sincere slow-formed conviction of what a British American policy should be—I look forward to the time when these Provinces, once united, and increasing at an accelerated ratio, may become a Principality worthy of the acceptance of one of the Sons of that Sovereign whose reign inaugurated the firm foundation of our Colonial liberties. If I am right, the Railroad will give us union—union will give us nationality—and nationality, a Prince of the blood of our ancient Kings. These speculations on the future may be thought premature and fanciful. But what is premature in America? Propose a project which has life in it, and while still you speculate, it grows. If that way towards greatness, which I have ventured to point out to our scattered communities be practicable, I have no fear that it will not be taken, even in my time. If it be not practicable, well, then, at least, I shall have this consolation, that I have invited the intelligence of these Provinces to rise above partizan contests and personal warfare to the consideration of great principles, healthful and ennobling in their discussion to the minds of men." ·

On the same subject, we find in a speech delivered at an earlier day in the Legislative Assembly, the following passage, in which Mr. McGee eloquently grouped in one view the main points of his magnificent picture :

"I conclude, Sir, as I began, by entreating the house to believe that I have spoken without respect of persons, and with a sole single desire for the increase, prosperity freedom and honor of this incipient Northern Nation. I call it a Northern Nation —for such it must become, if all of us do our duty to the last. Men do not talk on this continent of changes wrought by centuries, but of the events of years. Men do not vegetate in this age, as they did formerly in one spot—occupying one portion. Thought outruns the steam car, and hope outflies the telegraph. We live more in ten years in this era than the Patriarch did in a thousand. The Patriarch might outlive the palm tree which was planted to commemorate his birth, and yet not see so many wonders as we have witnessed since the constitution we are now discussing was formed. What marvels have not been wrought in Europe and America from 1840 to 1860 ? And who can say the world, or our own portion of it more particularly, is incapable of maintaining to the end of the century the ratio of the past progress ? I for one cannot presume to say so. I look to the future of my adopted country with hope, though not without anxiety.· I see in the not remote distance one great nationality, bound, like the shield of Achilles, by the blue rim of Ocean. I see it quartered into many communities, each disposing of its internal affairs, but all bound together by free institutions, free intercourse, and free commerce. I see within the round of that shield the peaks of the Western Mountains and the crests of the Eastern waves, the winding Assiniboine, the five-fold lakes, the St. Lawrence, the Ottawa, the Saguenay, the St. John, and the basin of Minas. By all these flowing waters in all the valleys they fertilize, in all the cities they visit in their courses, I see a generation of industrious, contented, moral men, free in name and in fact—men capable of maintaining, in peace and in war, a constitution worthy of such a country !"

There are, moreover, throughout the volume of speeches and addresses on "British American Union," passages which appear to be as reverent in their character, as they are eloquent in their language. We deeply regret that our space does not allow us to lighten this sketch with extensive extracts from Mr. McGee's writings. The manner, for example, in which the political and social systems of the United States re-act upon one another is frequently pointed out with graphic power. He might, though we do not know that he did, warn his readers that liberty in America may become, for there is great danger of her becoming, a suicide ; and expiring wretchedly from some act of unpremeditated violence ; for authority, as it has been truly said, is as necessary to the preservation of liberty as judges are to the administration of law. No violence therefore is done either to sentiment or experience in asserting, that they are most vigilant for freedom, who are most conservative of authority. After this manner Mr. McGee spoke, in closing his speech on the motion for an address to Her Majesty in favor of Confederation:

"We need in these Provinces, and we can bear a large infusion of authority. I am not at all afraid this constitution errs on the side of too great conservatism. If it be found too conservative now, the downward tendency in political ideas which characterizes this democratic age is a sufficient guarantee for amendment. Its conservatism is the principle on which this instrument is strong, and worthy of the support of every colonist, and through which it will secure the warm approbation of the Imperial authorities. We have here no traditions and ancient venerable institutions—here, there are no aristocratic elements hallowed by time or bright deeds—here, every man is the first settler of the land, or removed from the first settler one or two generations at the farthest—here, we have no architectural monuments calling up old associations—here, we have none of those old popular legends and stories which in other countries have exercised a powerful share in the Government—here, every man is the son of his own works. (Hear, hear!) We have none of those influences about us which elsewhere have their effect upon Government, just as much as the invisible atmosphere itself tends to influence life, and animal and vegetable existence. This is a new land—a land of young pretensions, because it is new—because classes and systems have not had time to grow here naturally. We have no aristocracy, but of virtue and talent—which is the best aristocracy, and is the old and true meaning of the term. (Hear, hear!) There is a class of men rising in these colonies superior in many respects to others with whom they might be compared. What I should like to see is—that fair representatives of the Canadian and Acadian aristocracy should be sent to the foot of the Throne with that scheme, to obtain for it the Royal sanction—a scheme not suggested by others or imposed upon us—but one, the work of ourselves, the creation of our own intellect, and of our own free, unbiassed, untrammelled will. I should like to see our best men go there, and endeavor to have this measure carried through the Imperial Parliament—going into Her Majesty's presence, and by their manner, if not actually by their speech, saying—"During Your Majesty's reign we have had Responsible Government conceded to us; we have administered it for nearly a quarter of a century, during which we have under it doubled our population, and more than quadrupled our trade. The small colonies which your ancestors could hardly see on the map, have grown into great communities. A great danger has arisen in our near neighborhood; over our homes a cloud hangs dark and heavy. We do not know when it may burst. With our strength we are not able to combat against the storm, but what we can do, we will do cheerfully and loyally. We want time to grow; we want more people to fill our country—more industrious families of men to develope our resources; we want to increase our prosperity; we want more extended trade and commerce; we want more land tilled—more men established through our wastes and wildernesses; we, of the British North American Provinces, want to be joined together, that if danger comes, we may support each other in the day of trial. We come to Your Majesty, who has given us liberty, to give us unity—that we may preserve and perpetuate our freedom; and whatsoever charter, in the wisdom of your Majesty and of your Parliament you give us, we shall loyally obey and observe, as long as it is the pleasure of your Majesty, and your successors, to maintain the connection between Great Britain and these Colonies."

An opponent of every kind of sectionalism, Mr. McGee was accustomed to say that he neither knew nor wished to know where the boundary is which divides Upper from Lower Canada. To him the whole was Canada. Rather than occupy himself in discovering boundaries, he worked hard to remove the pickets which separated the British Provinces from one another, that he might strengthen the barriers which protected them from the American States. He strove to weld them together by such bonds as love forges when he desires to fuse indissoluble ties. Therefore he advocated a policy of conciliation, a policy of forbearance, a policy of defence, a policy of commerce, a policy of intercourse, a policy of justice, a policy of peace; where men's thoughts should be charitable and their lives generous. He professed a statesman's anxiety not to re-enact in Canada the curses which have afflicted Ireland. With this purpose in view, it was his aim to discourage all societies whose objects were politically to separate men from one another, to discourage all brotherhoods whose rules cast men into antagonist associations, or sorted them into many-colored coteries, to breed suspicion and create enmity. He believed that there could be unity in plurality, and that the United Provinces like the United Kingdom, though made up of several races, might be tempered and welded into a State, one and indivisible.

Mr. McGee was not only a statesman and an orator—he was also, as most people are aware, a lecturer of no ordinary gifts, and an author of no ordinary ability. His range of subjects in the former character is perplexingly extensive, and suggests the notion that the nooks and crannies of his gifted brain must have been as thickly peopled with thoughts as were the tenements of the fifth and sixth wards of New York, with his ill-treated and closely-packed countrymen. To many of us it is a matter of regret that we know nothing more of those lectures than their names.* With respect

---

*The subjects include papers on Columbus, Shakespeare, Milton, Burke, Grattan, Burns, Moore, The Reformation, The Jesuits, The English Revolution of 1688, The Growth and Power of the Middle Classes in England, The Moral of the Four Revolutions, The Irish Brigade in the service of France, The American Revolution, The Spirit of Irish History, Will and Skill.

to Mr. McGee's works, we shall in this place content ourselves with a list of their titles only.*

Mr. McGee left Ireland for the second time in 1848. He returned to Ireland for the second time in 1865. Between that coming and that going, his personal history had been stamped with strange vicissitudes, and his political opinions had undergone serious changes. He left Ireland as a fugitive because failure had waited upon folly ; and he was then and for a long time afterwards obli-vious to every recollection but the self-evident one of failure. He returned to Ireland as an ambassador, because folly had been exor-cised by wisdom, and endeavor had been crowned with success. More-over, there was frankness in the confession, that he could think of his previous failure, if not with complacency, at least without either regret or shame. On both occasions he was equally sincere, and perhaps even when he was most wrong, he was most in earnest. It was not, however, as a private, much less as an obscure individual, that he was required to re-visit his native land. He did so by command of the Queen's representative, as a Commissioner from Canada. He did so, furthermore, as a member of the Executive Council for the purpose of joining his colleagues in conference with the repre-sentatives of Her Majesty's Government. When last in Ireland he took the opportunity of publicly explaining to his countrymen the true position, actual and comparative, of the Irish race in America, and he has become a martyr to the truth of his explanation. Nevertheless, the force and originality of the statements and opi-nions contained in his eloquent and celebrated Wexford speech, attracted unusual attention. The press and public men of Great Britain and Ireland had much to say of the speaker and his speech ; and no wonder, for recent events have taught them, and they have cruelly taught us in characters dripping red, that there was in what he said prophetic, as well as philosophic, truth.

---

* O'Connell and his Friends, 1 vol., Boston, 1844 ; The Irish Writers of the Seven-teenth Century, 1 vol., Dublin, 1856 ; Life of McMurrough, 1 vol., Dublin, 1847 ; Memoir of Duffy, Pamphlet, Dublin, 1849 ; Historical Sketches of Irish Settlers in America. 1 vol., Boston, 1850 ; History of the Reformation in Ireland, 1 vol., Boston, 1852 ; Catholic History of North America, 1 vol., Boston, 1852 ; Life of Bishop Maginn, 1 vol., New York, 1856 ; Canadian Ballads, Montreal, 1 vol., New York, 1858 ; Popular History of Ireland, 2 vols., New York, 1862 ; Notes on. Federal Governments, past and present, Pamphlet, Montreal, 1864 ; Speeches on British American Union, London, 1865.

In his personal appearance, Mr. McGee was what our portrait represented him to be. The photographer and the sunbeam seem to have understood one another admirably, when they turned Mr. McGee upside down in the camera; for he came out of the trial with incomparable exactness. The shadows of the outward man have been caught with felicitous accuracy. The intellectual man, if reproduced at all, must be reproduced by resorting to a process analogous to that which has been observed by the artist with respect to the physical man. Light from without enables us to see what Mr McGee was naturally. Light from within must enable us to see what he was intellectually. The mirror work of his mind is reflected in his words, and they who would examine its brightness, must do so in the pages of his writings.

The great gifts of genius which Divine Providence occasionally bestows, are, we believe, conferred as special trusts, for special uses. The subject of our sketch may have been, perchance he was, a chosen trustee of special gifts. He worked as if within the folds of the scheme which he had set himself to accomplish, there were many purposes of wisdom and charity. Directly, he desired by means of Confederation to bring about the intimate union of several Provinces. Indirectly, he desired by a policy of conciliation, to bring about the fusion of various races, and thus to supplement the law which shall create a new nation, with a policy which shall create a new nationality.

Nor are such plans purposeless, or such hopes chimerical. The races which inhabit British America represent peoples whose countries are made up of various tribes and different languages. The laws of moral like those of physical gravitation have not ceased to operate. The smaller bodies will be attracted, and eventually absorbed by the larger ones. What the United Kingdom is, the United Provinces will become. The question is one of time, and not of legislation. But the process of transition to be accomplished wisely, must be accomplished without violence and especially without wrong. The pursuit of such a purpose is worthy of a Christian statesman, and a philosophic patriot. Mr. McGee and the late Sir E. P. Taché were in their lives members of the same government and co-laborers in the same cause. With many others they sought to give shape and consistency to the vision of " a fraternal era," which each foreshadowed, which both foresaw, and which the most experienced of our statesmen are striving to bring about. Time will, we believe, approve such efforts ; and if success should crown exertion, many good men will envy, and all good men will praise them. If they fail, though there should be no such word as failure, the disappointment will, so far as their memories are concerned, be associated in either case with

> "A peace above all other dignities,
> A still and quiet conscience."

And in the possession of a "still and quiet conscience" the gifted orator and brave patriot, the Honorable Thomas D'Arcy McGee, has in this world won "dignities ;" and in the world to come, where "good deeds are had in remembrance," we doubt not he has found peace. It is hard to dwell on the ruthless character of the act which has given to eternity one, with reverence be it said, whose life was so valuable to time. It is idle, and per- chance wrong, to challenge His decrees without whom even a spar- row falls not ; and yet all intelligence is at fault, all reasoning vain as we mournfully recall his memory, who was so great, and so greatly feared ;·so great, and so greatly loved. Alas ! the "dome of thought" is crushed, "the golden bowl is broken."

> "Ay ! broken by a fiendish hand,
> Impell'd by fiendish thought ;
> . Seek not, oh ! man, to understand
> Why such a wreck was wrought ;

why in the meridian of his age, in the zenith of his usefulness ; scarcely beyond the morning of his fame, and only in the dawn of his honors, should his bright career have been brought to such a cruel end ? It is vain to ask, and impossible to answer such ques- tions. The blood-stained facts were related by different persons in nearly the same words, and in similar phrases telegraphed to different parts of the world. Thus the tidings read :

"OTTAWA, April 7th, 3.00 A.M.

"Mr. McGee left the House of Commons before two o'clock this morning, the moon making it nearly as light as day. He was accompanied by Mr. McFarlane, also a member of the House.

They separated at the corner of the street and went opposite ways
to their respective lodgings. When they said " good night" Mr.
McGee was not more than one hundred yards from his hotel.
He was smoking a cigar and carried his walking stick under his
left arm. To the " good night, Sir" of one of the humbler servants
of the House of Commons he answered cheerfully, " rather say
good morning ; for it is morning now." Such were his last words,
very simple words to be sure, but not without a meaning, suggestive
as we read them, of the day without night on which he was about
to enter. His right hand was occupied in finding the latch
key wherewith it was his practice to pass through the private
door, to his rooms. It is conjectured that as he stooped to place
the key in the door, an assassin from some place of convenient
concealment, shot him from behind, placing the muzzle of the pistol
very near to his head. The ball came out of his mouth destroying
his front teeth and burying itself in the framework of the door, and
from the nature of the wound, causing instant death. The pes-
tilent breath of the miscreant must momentarily, at least, have
mingled with his victim's, for they were apparently in such close
proximity as to cause the hair of the latter to be singed and the
flesh scorched by the flash of the shot. Thus was " the golden bowl
broken," and thus were scattered the garnered treasures of his
seething brain ; scattered, too, when he was actively coining
bright thoughts of sterling value to the country of his adoption,
as well as to the country of his birth."

It is difficult for those who have observed him closely and knew
him well, to hold a steady pen or write with calmness, much less
with coherency, of his great intellectual powers ; neither it is easy,
with the music of his melodeous voice still vibrating in our ears, to
speak of aught else than of the marvellous skill with which he
could pour out his soul in language most felicitously chosen ;
and yet it is desirable not to overlook a personal achievement
of still higher merit and perhaps of more difficult attainment,
viz : his triumphant, moral mastery of himself. We may refer now
with pride and thankfulness and without either shame or shock, to
the earnest character of his efforts to bring about an exact correspondence between his precepts and his example, between the tastes
that injured him, and the teachings that benefited others. It was

no easy trial for one of his exuberant mirth, his social predilections, and his convival habits, to lay aside the evil which had become associated with such experiences, and yet retain the experiences apart from the evil ; to preserve the relish for the friendship, and yet put from him the wine which he had esteemed as the almost inseparable associate of such friendship : to get rid of what theologians term the " besetting sin," and yet retain the grace and brightness of the virtue which is too commonly degraded by the sin.   Mr. McGee did so, and as we are informed, without resorting to any stimulating test, or to any public pledge ; but by bending his strong will to the vow which he had registered in the cloister of his soul, and which he had reverently presented to the supreme source of strength.   " I have made my resolve," said he to his attending physician, who, despairing of his life, recommended him to take some stimulants.   " I have made my resolve, and not to save life itself will I break through it."   He lived long enough to convince the most incredulous that he had won this great victory over himself, a victory which he had striven to win with the energy of despair, and for which his truest friends had labored with the earnestness of devotion.   His self denial, and their exertions were at length rewarded, and from thenceforward fear gave place to hope that his mental strength would not again be impaired by moral weakness.   When he was so unconsciously drawing near the close of his life, it is a blessed fact to remember and a holy one to record, that the follies and stains which had disfigured that life, one after another, had been overcome and cast out, leaving him at the last " renewed, regenerate, and disenthralled " by the threefold powers of virtue, temperance, and charity.

To return to our narrative.   Many of our readers are aware that when in Ireland about two years ago Mr. McGee made his celebrated Wexford speech.   That speech attracted towards him no small amount of attention on the part of the public men of England, and, we may add, no small amount of aversion on the part of the fiendish fraternity, whose machinations were so eloquently described and so fearlessly exposed.   Incidentally, and in his private capacity, he was encouraged to represent his views on the policy which English statesmen should observe in the government of Ireland ; and it is probable that such representations may have given rise to the opinion which the Earl of Mayo lately expressed in the House of Commons, when his Lordship is reported to have said that Mr. Thomas D'Arcy McGee was one of the ablest men in Canada—" a man who never speaks without influencing large masses of his countrymen wherever he addresses them, is at this moment one of the most eloquent advocates of British rule and British institutions to be found on the face of the globe." To his countrymen, if we recollect aright, Mr. McGee said on that occasion—" there ought to be no separation of the Kingdoms of Great Britain and Ireland. Each country would suffer loss in the loss of the other, and even liberty in Europe would be exposed to the perils of shipwreck if those islands were divided by a hostile sea." To Englishmen, he said, " try kindness and generosity in your legislation for Ireland. Treat Ireland as you have treated Scotland—consider her feelings, and respect her prejudices—study her history, and concede her rights—try equal justice to all—practice the golden rule and " do as you would be done by. Then will Irishmen in Ireland resemble Irishmen in Canada, where the Celt is not envious of the Saxon, and the Saxon is not supercilious to the Celt." Whether or not Mr. McGee's representations produced any effect on the minds of those to whom they were addressed, we have no means of knowing ; still, it is noteworthy that the policy in regard to Ireland which seems to find most favour at the present time very much resembles the policy, based on equal rights and equal respect for all origins, all races, and all creeds which he was accustomed to advocate, and which he is understood to have submitted to influential statesmen at home, when the opportunity was afforded to him of making a representation of his views. Fortunately, we have Mr. McGee's exposition of his course on this matter in his well remembered speech delivered at Ottawa on the 17th March last, the anniversary of his patron Saint, the last it was his lot to celebrate :

" Mr. Mayor, before I sit down—as this is St. Patrick's night, and I am the guest of the Irish citizens of Ottawa—if you will permit me, I may be expected to add a few general remarks on the critical subject of the state of the native land of our hosts and myself—the condition and state of Ireland. If I have avoided, for two or three years, much speaking in public on the subject of Ireland, even in a literary or historical sense, I do not admit that I can be fairly charged in consequence with being either a sordid, or a cold-hearted Irishman. I utterly deny, because I could not stand still and see our peaceful, unoffending Canada invaded and deluged in blood, in the abused and unauthorized name of Ireland, that, therefore, I was a bad Irishman. I utterly deny the audacious charge, and I say that my menta labors will prove, such as they are, that I know Ireland as well, both in her strength and her weakness, and love her as dearly, as any of those who, in ignorance of my Canadian position—in ignorance of my obligations to my adopted country—not to speak of my solemn oath of office—have made this cruelly false charge against me. You have been kind enough, Mr. Mayor, to allude to my 'History of Ireland.' No one is more sensible of its many deficiencies than I am, and if I live I hope to remedy some of them; but it certainly was to me a labor of love, and I believe it is the first time that a history of Ireland has ever been commenced and completed by a person situated as I was at the time, in a distant colony, after his personal connection with the mother country might be supposed to have closed forever. * * * * * * * * * * * *

As to Irish public affairs, I will further take the liberty to mention that when in 1865 and 1867, by the consent of my colleagues and my gallant friend here (Sir John A. Macdonald) I went home to represent this country, I, on both occasions—in 1865 to Lord Kimberly, then Lord Lieutenant; and last year to the Earl of Derby, whose retirement from active public life, and the cause of it, every observer of his great historical career must regret—I twice respectfully submitted my humble views and the result of my considerable Irish-American experiences, and that they were courteously, and I hope I may say favorably, entertained. I urged on those eminent statesmen in very homely words that they were keeping a pot boiling in Ireland to scald us out here in the colonies. Of course I do not admit, and never will admit, that any wrong done in Ireland, anciently or lately, can make an armed attack on our peaceful Canadian population anything else than methodized murder, or can entitle those taken red-handed in the fact, to any other judicial fate than that of marauders and murderers. But apart from our own recent experience, I felt it my duty to press the trans-Atlantic consequences of the state of Ireland on the attention of those who had the initiation of the remedy in their own hands, believing that I was doing Ireland a good turn in the proper quarter. I cannot accuse myself of having lost any proper opportunity of doing so, and if I were free to publish some very gratifying letters in my possession, I think it would be admitted by most of my countrymen, that a silent Irishman may be as serviceable in some kinds of work as a noisy one. I shall not presume, Mr. Mayor, because I am your chief guest, to monopolise the evening. I will only say further on the subject of Ireland, that I claim the right to love and serve her and her sons in Canada in my own way, which is not by either approval or connivance with enterprises my reason condemns as futile in their conception, and my heart rejects as criminal in their consequences.

"As for us who dwell in Canada, I may say finally, that in no other way can we better serve Ireland than by burying out of sight our old feuds and old factions, in mitigating our ancient hereditary enmities, in proving ourselves good subjects of a good government, and wise trustees of the equal rights we enjoy here, civil and religious. The best argument we here can make for Ireland, is to enable friendly observers at home to say, 'see how well Irishmen get on together in Canada. There they have equal civil and religious rights; there they cheerfully obey just laws, and are ready to die for the rights they enjoy, and the country that is so governed.' Let us put that weapon into the hands of the friends of Ireland at home, and it will be worth all the revolvers that ever were stolen from a Cork gunshop, and all the Republican chemicals that ever were smuggled out of New York."

C

Though not a delegate, Mr. McGee as a member of the Executive Council of Canada, was in a position to render his colleagues great assistance when they were engaged in carrying the act of confederation through the Imperial Parliament. The object which that act brought about was an object of absorbing interest to Mr. McGee, and without detracting from the wisdom or sagacity of any other statesman, we may perhaps say that his writings did much towards making the project popular in the minds, while his speeches made it pleasant to the hearts of men. Neither has the question found since then a more eloquent, a more consistent, or a more enthusiastic advocate than the subject of this sketch, for the purpose to which that question pointed had become the principle aim of his existence and the governing passion of his life. With his mind thus occupied Mr. McGee was appointed a Commissioner from Canada to the Paris Exposition, yet even there amidst the bewildering attractions of social and intellectual life, amidst the representatives of every tongue and tribe from " China to Peru," and encompassed with the surroundings of ancient and modern art, " in number without number,—numberless ;" yet even there, with such allurements and distractions, his best thoughts turned lovingly to that new Dominion whose foundation his industry had helped to lay, and whose superstructure his genius was assisting to build. His mind, though acutely alive to beauty and culture, nevertheless turned from the charms of Paris and the loveliness of France ; from the pleasant homesteads and profitable vineyards, from the intellectual wealth and heroic history of that alluring land ; to the seat of another sovereignty and the site of another empire—an empire,

> " Whose flanks were mighty oceans,
> Whose base the Northern pole."

From the central city of European civilization, the emporium of ancient art and the abode of modern fashion, he turned away his thoughts, and addressed his remarkable letter of the 1st May, 1867, to his constituents at Montreal, and through them to the inhabitants of Canada, and wisely counselled them after what manner they might hope to win a place in the family of states which few European nations had attained, and which none had surpassed. It was, we have reason to know, his intention to have supplemented that letter with another, but for reasons of a political, as well as of a personal kind, he deemed it advisable to postpone its publication.

The arrangements consequent on the formation of the first Privy Council of the new Dominion did not include a portfolio for Mr. McGee. To the regret of many persons and the surprise of all, he was, at his own generous and spontaneous desire, left out. The history of the transaction, so far as we are aware, has not been made public, but there can be no doubt whatever that Mr. McGee would not allow his personal wishes or his political claims to stand in the way of the harmonious action of the new experiment. His pride might have rebelled, or his poverty might have clamored, but honor and patriotism rebuked the one and silenced the other. He might have said, and probably did say, " don't consider me or my claims, look to the state and its welfare." Thus it chanced that the minister who was most generally known in the Maritime Provinces, and almost as well known in Ontario and Quebec, as any member of the administration, who had spoken more eloquently, and written more earnestly than any of his colleagues on the duties and advantages of union and confederation, waived all claim to be considered when that union was officially brought about, and the statesmen were chosen to give it consistency and put it in motion. No doubt the waiver was a sacrifice of feeling at the shrine of duty, but it is pleasant to know that it was unattended with any sacrifice of friendship. We believe indeed that moved by the generosity of his character, Mr. McGee withdrew his claim to office with such a steady purpose as to draw from Sir John A. Macdonald a remonstrance at the hurried character of the proceeding. By acting as he did, Mr. McGee thought to relieve Sir John of certain embarrassments. Nor was the supposition ill-founded, for it was said that his timely magnanimity overcame several very disturbing difficulties. Thus was it that the Minister of Justice and the Minister of Militia continued to be fast friends of Mr. McGee and he of them to the last hour of his life.

After the Privy Councillors were sworn in, new elections took place. It occasioned but small surprise to Mr. McGee that the felonious organizations which he had denounced when in England, and which he had sought to destroy on his return to Canada, exerted every influence they could command to exchange opposition and re-

sistance on their parts for assault and exposure on his. Like the
members of such associations, he knew something of secret organizations for violent purposes. He was not unacquainted with the mischievous character of the machinery by which such associations were
supported and kept in motion. He was not unfamiliar with the oaths,
or ignorant of the constitutions of such orders, and being in some
sort acquainted with their pernicious structure and dangerous tendency, he was enabled to speak with emphasis of things as they were,
and counsel with authority of things as they ought to be. But his
advice was received with contempt and his reproof was met with re-
sistance. The innocent blood so freely shed at Ridgeway provoked
neither compassion nor thought on their parts who shrank not from
the consequences of blood guiltiness. The Satanic league across
the southern frontier but too successfully impregnated certain localities in Canada with the sulphur of their sin. Being the largest
city of the Dominion, Montreal was supposed to contain the greatest
number of Fenian sympathisers, while the especial section which
Mr. McGee represented was regarded as the chosen seat of the
" Local Head Centre." While it was not possible for Mr. McGee
to have exaggerated the evil which such an organization was calculated to bring about, it is possible that he took an extreme view of
its local influence, and a mistaken one of the individuals by whom it
was sustained and defended. Thus when he somewhat rashly published what he knew, the disclosure fell far short of the public expec-
tation and peradventure of his own belief. He said either too much
or too little, and hence his reputation for acuteness acquired no
strength from what he then deemed it to be his duty to disclose.
The election which followed, though it resulted in a majority in his
favor of two hundred and eighty-four votes, shewed a serious defection in a certain class of his Irish supporters, and gave strength
to the belief that the leaven of mischief had by no means been
in-operative. It was a melancholy return of ingratitude, a base recom-
pense to one, who beyond all living Irishmen, had accomplished most
good for his country and his countrymen. But the wave of sedition
still flowed from the United States. In a public address at Buffalo,
within sight of the shores where many of our youth had without
provocation been foully slain, Senator Morrison, of Tennessee, is
reported to have said of those Irishmen, who would not enrol them-

selves in the fiendish enterprise which he favored and advocated, " the recreant traitors who refuse to join this organization will be handed down to posterity with the names of Benedict Arnold, Judas Iscariot, and D'Arcy McGee." If such words were spoken in the open, what might not have been determined upon in the secret councils of those who could coolly make covenants for blood? Underlying and concurrent with such allusions were ominous threats against his life, which, in various forms, but pointing to one issue, beset Mr. McGee almost everywhere. He was tracked and watched with such feline pertinacity as to induce his friends to place him and his house under the surveillance of the police. He was neither foolhardy nor insensible of the risk he ran, nor was he ignorant of the implacable character of the foes by whom he was surrounded. He had, however, long since settled his account with his conscience and determined irrespective of consequences to do his duty to his Sovereign, to his country and to himself. Nevertheless, as the Honorable Mr. Chauveau beautifully observed, even while he was thus pursuing the paths of charity, loyalty and honor, the shadowed hand of the assassin was upon him, pursuing him with that kind of stealthy craft with which the brute in his instinct hungers for the man.

By way of contrast to such savagery let us find a fitting place in this paper for Mr. McGee's sentiments on an act of atrocity which was but too typical of the crime by which he was to meet his death. The season selected was in both cases identical. It was the passion week of the Church Catholic. In one case the assassin chose Friday, the day whereon the atonement is commemorated. In the other, the assassin selected Tuesday, the eve of the betrayal. If no such panegyric has been pronounced on the Honorable Thos. D'Arcy McGee, as he pronounced on President Lincoln, it is because his mantle has not yet fallen on a competent successor. We shall suggest no contrasts, and draw no comparisons between the two events, for our readers will need little assistance in arriving at conclusions that may be damaging to our intellect, and must be degrading to our nature.

Hon. Mr. McGee rose to move the second resolution, and was received with loud cheers. He read the resolution:

"That we regard this unprovoked and most atrocious assassination, the greatest crime of our age, as committed not merely against the people of the United States, but against our common humanity, and against our common civilization."

He said:—Mr. Mayor and Gentlemen,—I am sure it is hardly necessary for me to say that I thoroughly and emphatically endorse every syllable contained in that short but expressive resolution. The awful crime which was committed on Friday night last in the city of Washington has thrilled through every heart in Canada, and but one universal sentiment—one universal sentiment without any exception, high or low.— prevails in relation to that crime. [Cheers]. That sentiment, in one view, expresses our horror and detestation of this cruel, cold-blooded assassination, and, in another, our deep, sincere sympathy with the nation, thus suddenly in the midst of its rejoicings, deprived by a ruthless murderer's hand of its kind-hearted chief magistrate. [Renewed cheers.] It is not on the principle of speaking no ill of the dead that I venture to subscribe personally to the declaration that this atrocious assassination is not only a crime against our common humanity, and our common Christian civilization, but that the loss of Mr. Lincoln at this moment is a loss to that humanity and that civilization. [Cheers.] The spirit of clemency, moderation, and of conciliation, displayed by the late President, were virtues uncommon, almost unexampled, in time of civil war; they are virtues whose sweet savor must have ascended before him to the judgment seat to which he was so suddenly summoned; they were virtues which entitled him to the beatitude pronounced upon a Judean mountain, and echoed all over heaven,—"blessed are the peace-makers." Let me venture to express the hope, Mr. Mayor, that as the American people revere the memory, so they will follow, in this respect, the sublime example of their lamented President. [Cheers.] To do otherwise—to lose their equilibrum—to forego their magnanimous purposes—even under the terrible shock they have suffered, would be to allow the assassin's policy to triumph over the policy of President Lincoln. (Continued cheers.) Thank God, there is one compensating consequence, attendant on even such a crime! Never yet did the assassin's knife reach the core of a cause or the heart of a principle. No wreath of Harmodious hides, in history, the barren results of these bloody short-cuts to forbidden ends. And as for the wretched criminals in this case—they cannot hope to escape their due punishment. They have conspired in what they have done against the whole civilized world, and the whole civilized world is concerned, and expended upon the guilty; but in the name of that humanity and civilization which mourned the fate of the murdered President; by the memory and example he left to his people, let the avenger's arms descend only on the guilty, and after due evidence of their guiltiness. (Cheers.) Should this be the course taken by the United States, I have no hesitation in saying that their greatest victory is yet before them; that a victory greater than any one on the field of battle; that the more shining page in their annals is yet to be written; and that the noblest example of self-government the world has yet seen, is about to be set by those who will so endeavor to honor the memory of Abraham Lincoln, by walking in the way, and under the guidance of the spirit, of Abraham Lincoln. (Cheers.) And though not mentioned in the resolutions, the unity of which could not well be broken, it is right I should add that the citizens Montreal, and the whole people of Canada—from the least to the highest, from the least obtrusive to his Excellency the Governor General—indulge the hope that the Secretary of State (Mr. Seward) may still be spared to his country and his friends. (Cheers.)

As his strength permitted, Mr. McGee availed himself of several opportunities to inculcate his lessons of conciliation and peace, of generous consideration and mutual good will. Under various pretexts, to different persons, before antagonistic societies and contending coteries, the like duties were enforced. The text was ever the same—"Sirs, ye are brethren," the application at one time patriarchal, and at another apostolic, was at all times consistent. "See that ye fall not out by the way." "Bear ye one another's burdens," for by so fulfilling the law of Christ you will best discharge the obligations you owe to your confederated country. We read such councils and feel the friendly touch of his generous helping hand in his lecture on the "Mental outfit of the New Dominion." In his speeches at Ottawa on the last anniversary of his patron Saint; in his sketch of the history of English literature, in his speeches in Parliament, and especially in that last speech made by him just before the debate closed which immediately preceded the hush and silence of his silver tongue. Incidentally the question of the repeal of the Union between Canada and Nova Scotia, became a subject of conversation in the House of Commons, when Mr. McGee, true to his own convictions, and his mission of good will and peace, informed those who favored such a project that time would smooth difficulties and intercourse would heal discontent; that justice would overcome prejudice, and that simple kindness would at length triumph and make converts of all. It is a matter of congratulation that so fair a report of those last words was made. But had we possessed fore-knowledge, how keen would have been the hearing ear, how exact the untiring pen ! We shall transcribe the speech as revised by an able and painstaking reporter, and subsequently inserted in the *Ottawa Times :*

MR. McGEE'S LAST SPEECH IN THE HOUSE OF COMMONS.

(Delivered on the Night of Monday, April 6, 1868.)

I took objection, sir, this afternoon, to the motion which has stood for some days in the name of the hon. member for Wellington Centre, and which has now been introduced as an amendment, being taken up out of order. I did so, as I stated then, believing that such a discussion as it was likely to occasion would not be con-

ducive to the peaceful interests of the country, and the objection which I raised
has been sustained. That objection was made as much in the interest of the hon.
member himself as of any other of this country. And had he but availed himself
of the interval which had thus been offered him for the exercise of reflection, and
decided not to throw himself, as he has now done, into this Nova Scotia quarrel, I
believe, sir, that, in after years, he would not have failed to acknowledge the service
which I had rendered him. I believe that the hon. member, although he had spent
some time previously in opposing Confederation, came from the hustings as a
"fair trial man"—one of those pledged at his election to give the new system a fair
trial—and how is he fulfilling that pledge? He is seeking for subjects of irritation,
and not finding it advisable openly to oppose the principles of Union here, loses no
opportunity to strike below the belt—to deal a stab in the dark—and it is time
now that the mask should be torn from his face. In the honorable profession to
which he belongs there are certain applications in use, known to the faculty as
emollients. If, in the exercise of the duties of that honorable profession, he makes
such liberal emollient use of vinegar and gall as he here employs towards Confederation, all I can say is that his unlucky patients are sincerely to be pitied. The
hon. gentleman had affected to be a convert to Confederation. If he had been
really a convert, he would be prepared even at the eleventh hour—even at the
eleventh hour and the fifty-ninth minute—to give the new system a fair trial. If
he had been earnest in his professions of desire for the success of Confederation he
might have said, "I do not think Dr. Tupper was the best choice for this mission,
but, since he has gone, I wish him all success for the sake of the welfare of the
Union." If he thinks it necessary at all to go into the matter of the appointment
of a gentleman to watch the interests of the Dominion in this matter of repeal, he
might be expected to do so in some such spirit, and to discuss it in some such tone.
He knows well that no good can possibly result from such a motion at such a time;
he knows well that the motion must certainly miscarry; and he knows well that
if it were possible for it to be adopted, the recall of Dr. Tupper would have no ap-
preciable effect in the conciliation of Nova Scotia. Why, sir, it would be only the
abstraction of a thimblefull from the bucket of her discontentment. The dissatis-
faction with the Union which unhappily prevails among a considerable portion of
the people there, is founded on other grounds than Dr. Tupper's appointment, and
has existed long previously. It is a family matter which it is right to leave within
the family; and it is for this reason that none other than a Nova Scotian could
have been judiciously chosen for the mission. There are not many in this House,
not Nova Scotians, who know much about Nova Scotia, and why not leave Nova
Scotians to meet Nova Scotians on their own ground? Dr. Tupper's character has
been assailed, and he himself personally maligned, and it is due to him that he
should be placed in a position to justify his conduct, with regard to the part he
had taken towards obtaining that Imperial Act of legislation by which the Union
had been established. It has been charged against him that he has lost the confidence of his own people. Sir, I hope that in this House mere temporary or local
popularity will never be made the test by which to measure the worth or efficiency
of a public servant. (Hear, hear.) He, sir, who builds upon popularity builds upon
a shifting sand. He who rests simply on popularity, and who will risk the right
in hunting after popularity, will soon find the object he pursues slip away from
him. It is, sir, in my humble opinion, the leader of a forlorn hope who is ready to
meet and stem the tide of temporary unpopularity, who is prepared, if needs be, to
sacrifice himself in defence of the principles which he has adopted as those of truth
—who shows us that he is ready not only to triumph with his principles, but even
to suffer for his principles—who has proved himself, above all others, worthy of

peculiar honor. (Applause.) It would show but a base spirit to sacrifice the man who had sacrificed himself for the Union. Nothing in this appointment has so greatly pleased me as the chivalry of spirit by which it has been dictated, and in which the hon. and learned Knight at the head of the Government has defended the hon. member for Cumberland in his absence. (Hear, hear.) I think, sir, that it is a pity that our Nova Scotia friends have not yet been able to make up their minds to give the scheme of Union a fair trial—that they have not consented to allow it to work untrammelled—that they have not been contented to watch its natural revolution in its appointed orbit unchecked by any stumbling block of their placing. For their own sakes—for the sakes of the ancient and renowned loyalty of their Province—I regret the course they have chosen. The Repeal address which the popular branch of their Legislature has adopted, and a copy of which is asked for in the motion now before us, is too school-boy a performance to prove creditable to Nova Scotia, on the journals of this House, if it is to be entered there. It is unworthy of that Province which has produced so illustrious an array of men of eminence—men whom we respect not only as lawyers of excellence, but also as acknowledged masters of English composition. It is a document at once ill-considered and fallacious—the production of empiric politicians—and, while we admit the discredit which its publication will attach to Nova Scotia, we must remember that any shortcoming on her part will reflect some portion of its discredit upon ourselves also, recollecting that whatever reputation is achieved by British Americans abroad, will be made applicable to every section of the whole Dominion. The propositions which the address enunciates are of two classes: firstly, statements of opinions or conclusions of argument which I, sir, for one, maintain to be unsound; and secondly, allegations of fact, which, in many instances, I know to be incorrect. And I say that it is not creditable to the author of that address to hear the tone in which he speaks of the administration of our institutions, and stigmatizes the Lieutenant-Governors who rule these Provinces as the mere tools of the Canadian Government, while he brands the Senators of his own Province as hirelings purchased to carry out the Union. It is not creditable that such a charge should have been brought by Nova Scotians against Nova Scotians. The address complains generally of injuries supposed to have been inflicted upon Nova Scotia by the old Province of Canada, and charges our statesmen with having juggled Nova Scotia out of her liberties. Such allegations or any allegations of the existence of any quarrel between Nova Scotia and Canada, are totally groundless. The address totally mis-states the question. The quarrel, if any quarrel there be, rests between Nova Scotia and the British Empire, from whose power the Act of Union alone derives its authority. And I think, sir, without any disrespect to that Province, that, in any controversy with the British empire, even the most patriotic Nova Scotian will admit himself overmatched in his attempt to limit the power of British influence. The Nova Scotian complaints divide themselves under two heads. A portion of them may be within the power of this House to remedy, and a portion of them are not so, but rest entirely with the Imperial Parliament. With the latter we have no concern, but, as regards our own share, I am sure that this House has no disposition to act in any spirit of unfairness. (Hear, hear.) It may be that there are some grounds of complaint with regard to some of the legislation of the early part of the session, and that, in such minor matters as the newspaper postage and certain tariff impositions, Nova Scotia may have some grounds for remonstrance, but so long as these points admit of modification or adjustment there will be no danger of its denial here. Whenever, sir, the Nova Scotian case on these issues, is presented fairly and calmly, it will find an amount of support here which.

will leave none of its advocates ground for complaint that the voice of Nova Scotia demanding justice is not fairly listened to within these walls. Then as now, and in that case as in every case, the representatives of Nova Scotia will find all parties in the House united in the desire of doing justice to their Province. And, sir, I am sure that not one of them will deny to-day that the same justice has been meted out to themselves as to all other portions of the Dominion, or that fear, favor or affection for any individual localities has been evinced in the Government of the Confederation. But Nova Scotia must only ask us to consider these subjects from a broad national point of view, and to deal with herself, not with exceptional partiality, but in the same spirit of even-handed fairness which we extended equally to Quebec, Ontario, or New Brunswick. And here, sir, I cannot withhold my acknowledgement of respect and appreciation of the moderate and large-minded, and truly national spirit, in which the hon. member for Lambton, the leader of the largest section of the Opposition, has approached and has dealt with all these great questions affecting the carrying out, and the maintenance and the welfare of the Union. All that can be justly required on the part of Nova Scotia, is that the opinions of her representatives, expressed in this Legislature here, shall carry with them their duly proportionate weight, and I have only to regret that gentlemen opposite should have taken their stand upon a platform so ultramontaine as to forbid approach by any well wisher of the Union. If there is to be any satisfactory co-operation upon the subjects in which they are most deeply interested, they must endeavor to modify the extremeness of their views—not necesssarily to compel to a coincidence with ours, but at least to present them, where alone argument or comparison can be possible, in the same plane. In the attitude they have taken, the first advances towards mutual political amity must come from them, and these advances will be, I shall venture to assert for all on our side, frankly and fairly responded to. I hold, sir, in my hand a little volume, a pamphlet which has been recently issued, but which I shall take the liberty of recommending to every member of this House, as well worthy of his attentive perusal. It is entitled "Intercolonial Trade—our only safe-guard against disunion." Its author is Mr. Haliburton, whose happy manner of treating his important subject displays the great ability hereditary in his name. Mr. Haliburton is not, I believe, actively mixed up with politics, and undoubtedly handles his topic in no merely party style. From this reason alone the conclusions from his disinterested, impartial and unimpassioned point of view, adopted and published in the interests of the permanent prosperity of the country, must be regarded of greater weight, and of greater soundness than those of the framers of this address, which can work but a temporary mischief. And this pamphlet shows conclusively beyond doubt or cavil, that ought indeed to be sufficiently obvious to all—that the Union is not to be consolidated by any temporary conciliating concessions to evanescent popular prejudice —not by any momentary humoring, in this direction or that, or some particular local or sectional phase of public opinion—but by our constant, earnest and unremitting care of the commercial welfare and progress of the Province. And besides this attention and practical consideration, we need, above everything else, the healing influence of time. I have, sir, great reliance on the mellowing effects of time. It is not only the lime, and the sand, and the hair, and the mortar, but the time which has been taken to temper it. And if time be so necessary an element in so rudimentary a process as the mixing of mortar, of how much greater importance must it be in the working of consolidating the Confederation of these Provinces. Time, sir, will heal all existing irritations; Time will mellow and refine all points of contrast that seem so harsh to-day; Time will come to the aid of the pervading principles of impartial justice, which happily permeates the whole land. By and by Time will show us the Constitution of this Dominion as much cherished in the hearts of the people of all its Provinces, not excepting Nova Scotia, as is the British Constitution itself. And I do not despair, with the assistance of time, of seeing, by and by, the hon. member for Lunenburg himself converted into the heartiest supporter of Union within these walls, willing and anxious to perpetuate the system which he will find to work so advantageously for his own Province, and adopting the position of the hon. member for Guysboro' as that of the true and patriotic statesman. I will not, sir, believe that such anticipations are ill-founded, for I can find their precedent even in the history of Nova Scotia herself. When Cape Breton was annexed to Nova Scotia —annexed not by any Act of Parliament, but simply by an order of the King in Council, the people were so strongly opposed to the Union that they almost threatened rebellion. Well, sir, this took place as lately as 1820, and already time has brought with it its certain healing operations, and there is no question raised now of the advantages which the Union has conferred. There is no such question, because there has been no consequent injustice. The incorporated people have found that there is no desire to rob them of their liberties, and no disposition to treat them with unfairness. They see, what time shows them, that the Union was effected for their advantage, as well as that of their neighbors, and they are satisfied, because they find it working for both. And, sir, I have every confidence that we will similarly wear out Nova Scotian hostility by the unfailing exercise and exhibition of a high-minded spirit of fair play. It has been said that the interests of Canada are diametrically opposed to the interests of Nova Scotia, but I ask which of the parties to the partnership has most interest in its successful conduct, or has most to fear from the failure which the misfortunes or the losses of any of its members must occasion. Would it not be we who have embarked the largest share of the capital of Confederation? Our friends, sir, need have no fear but that that Confederation will ever be administered with serene and even justice. To its whole history, from its earliest inception to its final triumphant consummation, no stigma can be attached, no stain attributed. Its single aim from the beginning has been to consolidate the extent of British North America with the utmost regard to the independent powers and privileges of each Province, and I, sir, who have been, and who am still, its warm and earnest advocate, speak here not as the representative of any race, or of any Province, but as thoroughly and emphatically a Canadian, ready and bound to recognize the claims, if any, of my Canadian fellow-subjects, from the farthest east to the farthest west, equally as those of my nearest neighbor, or of the friend who proposed me on the hustings. (Great applause.)

And with such sentiments in his heart and with such words on his lips, his public life in Canada was brought to a consistent end. A few minutes later, and the assassin's bullet made space enough for his spirit to escape the thrall of the flesh; and alas! by the same act, to make a blank in our Legislature, and our literature, by destroying our most precious portion in the " Mental outfit of the New Dominion." Horror and indignation walked through our thoroughfares and grief found congenial articulation in the language of passion. " The fir tree howl'd, for the cedar had fallen." The press groaned with sorrow while on its teeming pages, passages bright with tears, bore eloquent testimony to the merits of the dead. But while the murderers had make a blank where the nation had found a prize, it was not in his power, in the power of the whole brotherhood of conspirators, to bury Mr. McGee's services in the shroud of blood, wherein they too successfully had buried him. The great duty which he had assigned to himself of consolidating and building up the British American confederacy will not be frustrated by his most inhuman murder. On the contrary, in studying his character as a statesman and his teachings as a scholar, even those who most opposed him will be charmed by his genius, touched by his charity, and moved by his example, to still their passions, to lay aside " their prejudices and their partial affections " to hush all fretful cries, and to banish all craven fears, and thus learn from his sacrifice and death, lessons as valuable, and perchance more availing, than those which he had taught in his life. The Government of the Dominion, the Legislatures of the Provinces, and the Corporations of Cities, seemed to vie with one another in the amount of the rewards which should be paid for the discovery of the murderer. In the meanwhile, the pavement where that pool of human blood lay was sacredly enclosed, no foot was allowed to cross it. It was left, some said, to cry to heaven for vengeance ; and others said that like the blood of a sacrifice, it was as an offering of peace to the wicked passions of men.

We shall insert what is without doubt the best report now extant of what followed later in the day.

HOUSE OF COMMONS.

OTTAWA, Tuesday, April 7th, 1868.

The SPEAKER took the chair at ten minutes past three.

The galleries were densely crowded.

Sir JOHN A. MACDONALD rose amidst the breathless silence of the House and manifesting feelings of the most profound emotion, which for some time almost stopped his utterance, said :—Mr. Speaker, it is with pain amounting to anguish that I rise to address you. He who last night, nay this morning, was with us and of us, whose voice is still ringing in our ears, who charmed us with his marvellous eloquence, elevated us by his large statesmanship, and instructed us by his wisdom and his patriotism, is no more—is foully murdered. If ever a soldier who fell on the field of battle in the front of the fight, deserved well of his country, Thomas D'Arcy McGee deserved well of Canada and its people. The blow which has just fallen is too recent, the shock is too great, for us yet to realize its awful atrocity, or the extent of this most irreparable loss. I feel, sir, that our sorrow, our genuine and unaffected sorrow, prevents us from giving adequate expression to our feelings just now, but by and by, and at length, this House will have a melancholy pleasure in considering the character and position of my late friend and colleague. To all, the loss is great, to me I may say inexpressibly so; as the loss is not only of a warm political friend, who has acted with me for some years, but of one with whom I enjoyed the intercommunication of his rich and varied mind; the blow has been overwhelming. I feel altogether incapable of addressing myself to the subject just now. Our departed friend was a man of the kindest and most generous impulse, a man whose hand was open to every one, whose heart was made for friendship, and whose enmities were written in water; a man who had no gall, no guile; "in wit a man, simplicity a child." He might have lived a long and respected life had he chosen the easy path of popularity rather than the stern one of duty. He has lived a short life, respected and beloved, and died a heroic death; a martyr to the cause of his country. How easy it would have been for him, had he chosen, to have sailed along the full tide of popularity with thousands and hundreds of thousands following him, without the loss of a single plaudit, but he has been slain, and I fear slain because he preferred the path of duty. I cannot but quote from his speech of last night. "Sir," said Mr. McGee, "I hope that in this House "mere temporary or local popularity will never be made the test by which to "measure the worth or efficiency of a public servant. (Hear, hear.) He, sir, who "builds upon popularity builds upon a shifting sand. He who rests simply on "popularity, and who will risk the right in hunting after popularity, will soon find "the object he pursues slip away from him. It is, sir, in my humble opinion, the "leader of a forlorn hope who is ready to meet and stem the tide of temporary "unpopularity, who his prepared, if needs be, to sacrifice himself in defence of the "principles which he has adopted as those of truth—who shows us that he is "ready not only to triumph with his principles, but even to suffer for his principles "—who has proved himself, above all others, worthy of peculiar honor." (Applause.) He has gone from us, and it will be long ere we find such a happy mixture of eloquence and wisdom, wit and earnestness. (Hear, hear.) His was no artificial or meretricious eloquence, every word of his was as he believed, and every belief, every thought of his, was in the direction of what was good and true. Well may I say now, on behalf of the Government and of the country, that, if he has fallen, he has fallen in our cause, leaving behind him a grateful recollection which will ever live in the hearts and minds of his countrymen. We must remember too that the blow which has fallen so severely on this House and the country will fall more severely on his widowed partner and his bereaved children. Of their sorrows I will not venture now to speak—but I would remind the House that he was too good, too generous to be rich. He hast left us, the government, the people, and the representatives of the people, a sacred legacy, and we would be wanting in our duty to this country and to the feeling which will agitate the country from one end to the other, if we do not accept that legacy as a sacred trust, and look upon his widow and children as now belonging to the State. (Hear, hear.) I now move that the House adjourn, and that it stand adjourned till Tuesday next, at half past seven.

Mr. McKENZIE said, in rising to second this motion, I find it almost impossible to proceed; but last night we were all charmed by the eloquence of our departed friend, who is now numbered with our honoured dead, and none of us dreamed when we separated last, that we should so very soon be called upon in this way to record our affection for him who had been thus suddenly cut off. It was my own lot for many years to work in political harmony with him, and it was my lot sometimes to oppose him, but through all the vicissitudes of political warfare we ever found him to possess personally that generous disposition so characteristic of the man and his country; and it will be long, as the Hon. Knight at the head of the Government has said, before we shall see his like again amongst us. I think there can be no doubt upon the mind of any one who has watched the events of last year in this Province, in connection with events in his own distant native land, that he has fallen a victim to the noble and patriotic course which he has pursued, and that he has been assassinated by one of those who are alike the enemies of our country and of mankind. (Hear, hear.) I cordially sympathise with all that has been uttered by the honorable' gentleman at the head of the Government, in making this motion, and I have no fear that the generosity of Canadians will fail when it comes to be considered what we owe to his memory, and what we owe to his family. I would gladly, if I could, speak for a few minutes regarding the position he held amongst us, during the few years he lived and laboured as a public man in this colony, but I cannot do more to-day than simply record my full appreciation of his public character as an orator, a statesman and a patriot, and express the fervent hope that his family thus suddenly bereaved of him who was at once their support and their shield, will not, so far as comforts of this life can be afforded, suffer by his death : and my desire is that all the consolation that can be given by those who were long his companions in public life may be afforded at this trying moment to his grief striken family, in the expression of our deep sympathy; as the sentiment of universal sorrow which touches every generous heart in the land will bring to his wife and children the general sympathies of the people. This is the first instance we have had in our country of any of our great public men being stricken down by the hand of the assassin, and grief for our loss, and grief for his family are mingled in my mind with a profound feeling of shame and regret that such a crime could, by any possibility, be perpetrated on our soil, and I can only hope that the efforts to be made by Government will lead to the discovery that to an alien hand·is due the sorrow that now clouds not only this house but the whole community. (Hear hear.)

Mr. CARTIER.—Mr. Speaker, I will state at the outset that my heart is filled with feelings of deepest sorrow. I had the pleasure and delight in common with all the members of this house, to listen last night to the charming eloquence of the representative of the city of Montreal, and no one expected at that moment, that any one of us should be here speaking to-day on such a lamentable evil as that which befell us immediately after the adjournment of the house. I feel deep regret at this moment that I am not gifted with that power of speech, that power of description, that power of eloquence, which distinguished our departed friend. I could make use of such power to bring back before you, sir, and before this house, in proper language the great loss we have suffered, the loss the country has suffered, and the loss mankind has suffered, in the death of Thomas D'Arcy McGee. (Hear, hear.) Our colleague, Mr. McGee, was not an ordinary man; he was, I may say, one of those great, gifted minds, whom it pleases Providence sometimes to set before the world, in order to show to what a height the intellect of man can be exalted by the Almighty. Mr. McGee adopted this land of Canada, as his country, but although this was the land of his adoption he never ceased to love his mother country, his dear old Ireland. In this adopted land of his he did all in his power in order that his countrymen should be rendered as happy as possible, whether their lot was cast in this country, in Ireland, or in any part of the globe where an Irishman had set his foot. Mr. McGee though very young had a great deal of experience. He was connected with political events in Ireland in 1848 and there is not the least doubt that those painful times caused him to give the deepest consideration to those political evils, though he was, as described by my honorable friend the leader of

Government, a man of impulse, of genius, and of wisdom, it is very seldom we meet a man on earth having those fine gifts who was so judicious as our late colleague. He was educated as it were for the benefit of his country. He is no longer among us, and I suppose all of my listeners at this moment will say with me that it has not been given to any one of us to have ever listened to so eloquent a public man. Every one of us shares the conviction that such happiness, such delight will never be given hereafter to any one of us during our life time. He has left us. He has left behind him expressions of his feeling of patriotism and an immense amount of evidence, that no Irishman, on earth, loved so much as he did dear Ireland. Mr. Speaker, I cannot but allude at this moment to that foreign organization in the land inhabited by our neighbors. 1 have not the least doubt that Mr. McGee, by warning the Irishmen of Canada not to join in that detestable organization, rendered the greatest service that an Irishman can render to his country. (Hear, hear.) He acquired for the Irish inhabitants of Canada the inestimable reputation of loyalty and of freedom from any participation in the hateful, detestable feelings and doings of the members of that abominable institution, the Fenian organization. (Hear, hear.) Now that he is no longer amongst us, that he has passed from life to death, it is very likely that his death was the work of an assassin in that organization. It is not for us at this moment to excite feelings of revenge against the perpetrators of such an abominable act, but every one of us knows this, that if Thomas D'Arcy McGee had not taken the patriotic stand which he took before and during the Fenian invasion of this country, he would not be lying a corpse this morning. At all events, sir, every Irishman inhabiting the different Provinces of Canada, when they consider the services Thomas D'Arcy McGee rendered to them in order to induce them not to partake in that Fenian movement in the United States, will lament his death as much as any one of us. Now, Mr. Speaker, I will not allude to his private qualities. I have known him; and we know that of t is world's goods he possessed very little. He was a poor man, but I know myself that feelings of charity swelled his heart. The little he had, he was always willing to share with his poor countrymen. Although he was so gifted, although he soared so high above the ablest man in the land, did he ever show a feeling of vanity, did he ever show, by even a word, that he was more gifted than any one else in the land? No! but he used all his great power and ability modestly, for the good of his native land and his adopted country. I do hope and trust that this great Dominion will not leave helpless his widow and his dear children. He has not fallen, it is true, upon the field of battle; it cannot be said that he met the fate of a military hero; but his end was that of a Parliamentary hero. For two or three years he knew the bad passions which existed among certain classes on the other side of the lines. Again and again he received, through newspapers and other means, warning of the fate which he met last night. Well, did that prevent him from continuing his good work of inducing his countrymen to have nothing to do with that detestable organization? No! he laboured on, and now that he is no longer amongst us, we feel that the Irish inhabitants of the Dominion will appreciate the services he has rendered to them, and that they will mingle their tears with ours for his irreparable loss. (Hear, hear.)

Mr. CHAMBERLIN said: When profound grief, such as now reigns in this House, weighs down men's hearts, few words are best. Yet I am loth that we should depart ere some tribute of respect has been paid, some word of regret uttered, even in this place, in behalf of the fraternity of letters, to which the deceased belonged. It is fit it should be spoken, even though it come from a member of what is held to be the lower branch of the literary craft to which I belong, in which, too, our deceased friend held it no mean honor to win a distinguished place.

(Hear, hear.) His love of letters, and the great diversity of his writings, are well known. Of his diligence in promoting the cause of literature, his endeavors to create a love of letters among the young men of Montreal and of the whole Dominion, it has been my privilege also to know much. He had made himself known in Canada and abroad as a lecturer, essayist, historian and poet with so much distinction that it may be said of him as was said of a celebrated countryman of his —"Nihil tetigit quod non ornavit." Others have spoken in fitting terms of the matchless oratory with which he clothed statesmanlike thought, and of his labors to allay intestine strife and promote the highest interests of the country, for which he has lost his life. But the press and literature of Canada must also mourn to-day for their brightest light extinguished; their greatest man prematurely reft from them, as he has been, from his country. (Applause.)

Mr. ANGLIN said: I would be unworthy of my position in the House if I did not take this occasion to join in the expressions of horror and detestation which I know every member of this House, every man worthy of the name of a man, in this Dominion, must feel at the atrocious crime which has been committed. (Hear, hear.) I feel peculiarly embarrassed on this occasion, because it has been assumed, and I fear only too correctly, that this foul assassination has been the work of an organization of Irishmen—not I trust of Irishmen belonging to this Dominion—though I think it will not require much intelligence to determine that any Irishman who has enjoyed the free institutions of this country could not be guilty of such a dastardly act, (hear, hear,) but I cannot help thinking nevertheless, that as wherever Irishmen are—they are all one people—the crime of one will reflect on them all. I think I may speak on behalf of the whole of the Irishmen of this Dominion, I am sure I may on behalf of those of my own province, in expressing our utter destestation of this crime. It is an outrage that will probably have a great effect on the future of this country. None of us can realize its effects yet, the shock is too recent, none of us can, on this occasion, give vent to the feeling which overmasters us. Perhaps after all this is the highest tribute which we can pay to the man who has gone from amongst us. This must be the most telling mode of showing to our countrymen what our feelings are, and that we all agree in stigmatizing a crime of this nature. (Hear, hear.) I go even further than those who have preceded me, and express the hope that the assassin shall be speedily brought to justice. Not that we shall indulge in feelings of vengeance, but that all the means at the command of the Government shall be put forth to ferret out this assassin wherever he may be concealed; that the death of Mr. McGee may be revenged, and that the supremacy of the law may be maintained. (Hear, hear.) I feel myself, Mr. Speaker, quite incapable of adequately expressing my feelings on this occasion, but I could not allow the opportunity to pass without saying these few words. (Applause.)

Mr. CHAUVEAU said: I also must pay my tribute of homage to him who has just fallen the victim of a crime of which we have truly said that it is without precedent in the history of our country. I recall the eloquent speech which he made even last night, in which one would search in vain for a single word, which could wound or irritate in the least degree, the feelings of those to whom he particularly addressed himself. (Hear, hear.) Those who heard him can bear testimony that the advice and counsels were not given with a spirit of provocation, but on the contrary, they were given in a spirit of conciliation and concord. Those who heard him can truly judge that this spirit animated him last night, in his remarks on the subject of Nova Scotia. They can remember that he terminated his speech in saying that he fervently hoped that the debate would not have any unfavorable results for the country, and would not produce any evils to this province. A like crime has happily no precedent in the history of our country, and were it possible for us to console ourselves for the loss which we have sustained in the death of a friend; of an eminent man—of the prince of orators; we would find that consolation in the glory and relation of his death. That death is the baptism in blood of Confederation, and the sacrifice of him who did so much to bring about that Confederation, is a fact which ought to raise us in our own estimation, and make us judge of the height of our mission. Though Mr. McGee has not fallen on the battle-field, his death is none the less glorious, because it is the consummation of a grand idea, a grand principle;—that of the union of the colonies. As the heroes on the field of battle, so the soldiers of grand causes are ever in danger. Great things are rarely done except at the peril of the lives of those who accomplish them, hence Mr. McGee's patriotism made him disdain that danger, neither did the fear of that danger ever caused him to recoil in the struggle which he had undertaken against those whose hand struck him last night. (Hear, hear.) Warnings to him had not been wanting, either publicly—through the press, or in the sinister form of threatening letters; but his great soul disdained those threats, and nothing deterred him from the great task which he had undertaken. Notwithstanding such menaces he pursued his patriotic course with fearless intrepidity. It is true indeed, that the assassin was not abashed by such courage for he watched him steadily and crept behind him that he might, coward like, with the greater certainty strike the fatal blow. Alas! there is reason to believe that the cruel monster was present at the last sitting of the House, aye and in those galleries heard the words of peace and good will that charmed us all, and yet he remainded unmoved by the persuasive power of such sentiments; unmoved, because his heart was full of evil and his mind was full of crime, and both were intent on blood—the blood of the benefactor of his country and his countrymen. Truly, if that death is a glorious one for the country, it is a sensible and terrible loss for his family. Even yesterday he presented a petition in favour of the representatives and the family of a hero, that of Colonel DeSalaberry. He told me what he proposed to submit, and to ask the House to come to the aid of the descendants of DeSalaberry, and a few hours later he himself fell as a hero and left a family without support, without hope, and without fortune. The name of D'Arcy McGee will live in the History of Canada, and his death will mark the death of Fenianism, for never has cause gained by assassination. No! from Julius Cæsar to Henry the Fourth, from Count Rossi to President Lincoln, never has a cause succeeded by assassination; for the death of those great men was the signal of the death of the cause of the party under the blows of which they fell, as the death of D'Arcy McGee will be the signal of the death of the party which exercised its vengeance on him. I think that the murder of the Hon. Mr. McGee will have a happy influence upon Canada, inasmuch as it will force that spirit of disloyalty heretofore prevalent to disappear, and inspire a horror of the party which gave it birth; while, at the same time, it will contribute to the glory and the greatness of Canada. It has been happily said, the Hon. Mr. McGee never displayed the least vanity, or prided himself upon his transcendent talents. He was always modest and affable towards all, and never appeared to appreciate his own merit. He also had a generous heart. He was always ready to contribute to every charity or charitable institution. I have often met him in Montreal in ceremonies and public celebrations got up for the purpose of doing good and instilling charity, and he never refused his aid or refused to draw on the eloquent fund of words which sprung from the bottom of his heart in aid of the poor. On these occasions he always seemed to be under the impression that he was only doing what another person would have done, and his good heart was equal to his modesty. The orphans and unfortunates have lost in him a great protector, but he also leaves behind him a widow and some orphans. To-day we must perforce deplore his death. To-morrow, or at another sitting of the House, we will have a duty to fulfil towards his memory and his family (hear, hear), and I am happy to see that the Government has already thought of an act of reparation, an act of justice; and I am sure that so far as the Province of Quebec is concerned, whatever sum the Government proposes, that Province will heartily concur in. The Hon. gentleman, whose speech was delivered in French, was visibly affected, and was listened to with marked attention.

Mr. E. M. MACDONALD (Lunenburgh, N. S.). Mr. SPEAKER,—When it is remembered that in the debate last night I was placed prominently in opposition to the honorable gentleman whose violent and tragical death has filled the members of this House with emotions of grief, I may perhaps be excused if I attempt briefly to add my tribute of respect to what has been said by those who have already spoken. I feel utterly unable, Mr. Speaker, adequately to express the feelings that at this moment almost overwhelm me. How little did I dream, when feebly attempting last night to combat his arguments, that I was to be his last opponent—how little did any of us suppose, when listening to his glowing periods scarce twelve hours ago, that we were listening to him for the last time. When we remember that the voice whose eloquent utterances have so often charmed this House is hushed forever—when we think that the active, teeming brain, whose prolific labors have left their impress upon the institutions and the literature of this country, has ceased to animate the form that yesterday was D'Arcy McGee, and is now but a mass of cold, senseless clay,—and when we reflect upon the heinous criminality of the act by which so valuable a life has been destroyed—in the presence of this recent horror men stand aghast, and detraction is dumb. It was my lot to be among those who viewed some political events from a different stand point from that occupied by the deceased; but whatever difference of opinion may have existed among public men as to the honorable gentleman's political views, on one point there was no difference—all were agreed in admiration of the great intellectual power, the genial kindliness of heart, and the expansive charity that characterized him whose loss we are now called on so suddenly to mourn, and who, now that he has gone from this House, has scarcely left his equal behind him. I feel, Mr. Speaker, that in the murder of Mr. McGee, a stigma has been cast upon the good name of British America, upon the people of every origin, who acknowledge allegiance to Great Britain on this continent; and that the honor of this legislature, and the honor of the Dominion, are involved in the duty of tracing out and bringing to punishment, the criminal who has been guilty of this foul deed.

Hon. STEWART CAMPBELL said: I cannot allow this opportunity to pass without a few observations. It affords me painful gratification to find that although on some occasions I may differ from the other representatives of Nova Scotia, on this occasion and on this grave topic we are in feeling in sympathy and in heart, one and the same. Sir, I feel assured when the intelligence of the sad and awful fact which has bowed us almost to the dust reaches that Province, that throughout its length and breadth there will be mourning and weeping, lamentation and woe. Mr. Speaker, the distinguished Statesman, whose untimely end we are now lamenting, was well known in that Province. His honored reputation had secured there many warm and sincerely devoted friends, not only of one class, but of all classes: the highest and the humblest alike appreciated and asserted his private and his public merits, and all are at this moment in solemn accord with the feelings and the utterances which now dignify this hour and this place. Sir, it is my misfortune that I had no very long personal acquaintance with the great departed : but that acquaintance was sufficiently long, and sufficiently privileged, to impress me with an abiding conviction of his various disinterested and patriotic services on behalf of the country in which his lot was cast, and which he loved so well. But if there were nothing else to attach me to his memory, it would be the recollection of the splendid exhibition of his eloquence, his patriotism, and his wisdom, as displayed on the floor of this House last night, only a brief period before his valuable life was so shockingly terminated. It was a valuable legacy, I fear, that the record of those precious sentiments, that exalted philosophy, that sound advice will not be adequately preserved. I would they could be deposited in the archives of this Dominion, and fondly cherished and treasured up in the hearts of its people. Mr. Speaker, it affords me the highest satisfaction to hear that it is the intention of the government to do what can be done to alleviate the pangs and privations of the widow and the children of our departed friend—they are to be left not to the charities of a cold world, but to the justice of an obligated country. Sir, I shall say no more. The eloquent lips of the greatest amongst us have been unequal to this occasion ; what then can be expected from me ? I can only cordially agree with the motion to adjourn the House.

It was a frightful novelty in Canada to see the walls of our highways stained with placards offering rewards for the discovery of assassins. Such sights made people pause and inquire whether it is inevitable that crime should travel hand in hand with civilization. Lately in the United States, and now in the British Provinces, the exceptional vices of the old world seemed to have taken root in the new. In one case striking a statesman eminent for his serene wisdom as well as his exalted position ; and in the other striking a statesman conspicuous alike for the generosity of his character and the greatness of his genius. Similar crimes were, as a matter of course, dealt with in a similar manner. Outraged society addressed itself to the duty of vindicating its violated order and of re-asserting the majesty of the law. The Governments of the Dominion and of the two Provinces of old Canada offered $10,000 reward for the discovery of the murderers. The Corporation of Ottawa, with praiseworthy unanimity, offered $4,000 for the conviction of the miscreants who had fixed such an accursed stain on the fair repute of the new capital. The City of Montreal lost no time in declaring its detestation of so foul a deed by promising $5,000 for the conviction of the perpetrator. The Police machinery of the whole Dominion was put in instant motion, and we may rest assured that the acute officers of that service will penetrate every haunt, and scour every crevice of infamy, until they shall bring the history of the crime to light and the authors of it to justice. Leaving the duty to those to whom it belongs of unmasking organized murderers, the public directed their attention to the sacred obligation of doing honor to the dead, and of providing for the comfort of those of his name and blood who had especial reason to mourn his loss. Mr. Walter MacFarlane of Montreal and other personal friends arrived at Ottawa charged with the duty of bearing Mr. McGee's remains to the former city, where preparations of no ordinary character were in progress to receive them, and in due time to bear them, with becoming solemnity, to their last resting place. The Corporation of Montreal had already determined that the funeral should be conducted with every ceremony which taste could devise and money command, and that the cost should be borne by the City Exchequer. All business was involuntarily suspended, for the troubled thoughts of the community could not flow peacably in their accustomed channels. People spoke incoherently, for indignation was mingled with dismay at the disgrace which had overtaken our civilization as well as the disaster which had befallen our country.

The newspapers very truthfully indicated the popular pulse, and shewed how acutely the heart of the whole community had been touched by the inexcusable crime. For, from every quarter, from town and city, from village and hamlet, the soul of the people sought and found expression in the language of poetic passion. Grief does not commonly articulate its misery in nicely balanced words, nor is it careful that its periods should be rounded with smoothness. The lament of the disconsolate will not satisfy the ear of indifference, nor will the wail of the bereaved be controlled by the exact rules of harmony. When the quick of sorrow is touched, the pain will be sharp enough to provoke a cry that all may hear, but which few will criticize. It was, therefore, natural that he who so pre-eminently possessed the divine gift of poesy, should, from his winding sheet of blood, have awakened in less gifted natures, passions akin to those which always moved him. It was homage and not ambition that caused such persons to graft their figurative rose on a furze bush, and bid it blossom in his praise. It was tribute and not rivalry which caused them to attune their ill-strung dulcimers to his well set harp ; and, by so doing to provoke if possible, a harmony they were unable to command. In metaphor and music, in rhetoric and song, they desired to honor the minstrel with the best instrument they had, for they knew the generosity of his nature, and remembered that his sympathetic soul was unaccustomed to meet such efforts with a sneer. The contributions in verse from bards of the backwoods, from Sandwich to Nova Scotia, though widely differing in poetic merit, are not unworthy of being preserved among those rough examples of human passion in which the stricken mind occasionally hymns its homage to the virtues of the living, or the merits of the dead.

The *Montreal Gazette* very truly observed that "Mr. McGee was the very apostle of peace. He taught us all, Protestant and Catholic, French and English, that we are brethren living in this our fair land, to enjoy it in all brotherly love with one another. And will his death dissolve this union? We trow not. A common sorrow is a good cement for love. The tears that fall on his tomb will be from the hearts of thousands, without distinction of race or of creed, tears that will bind the weepers together in love."

Such sentiments were common to the people of the whole Province, but they were especially present to the minds of his friends and constituents in the City of Montreal. Love and grief, indignation and vengeance, the tear of pity and the lust for blood, stirred passion to its very depths, while they united together, as one man, the whole population of one of the most cosmopolitan cities in the world. Men assembled as citizens and seemed to vie with one another in speaking his praises. English and French were there, Scotchmen and Irishmen, the Pole and the Swiss, Germans and Danes, Christians and Jews. The origins were diverse enough, but they agreed in opinion and were settled in their resolve. Then they separated as citizens and re-assembled as countrymen; again they divided, and again came together as members of different brotherhoods, according to their professions, their callings, or their trades; but no matter whether in the character of national, learned, or philanthropic societies, clubs for social purposes, or unions for trading purposes; the aim and object of every gathering was identical:—to pay fitting tribute to the memory of their murdered representative. The hives of every branch of industry sent out their swarms; seminaries of learning contributed their scholars. Catholic Christianity was represented in the persons of its accredited clergy, and Protestant Christianity by its chosen ministers. All met together to take common counsel on the way in which they could best do him honor who, in reverent imitation of the loftiest pattern, had striven to promote peace and good will among men. In the meanwhile, though his lifeless body lay " unanointed and unaneled," it was neither un-cared for nor unwept. For three days he lay in state, carefully watched by loving friends and sorrowfully looked at by mourning thousands. By the especial request of the community and the considerate permission of his widow, his house was open to all who desired to see him in that fatal sleep which a fiend brought about but which an angel will destroy.

In the meanwhile, people from all parts of the Dominion, and many from the United States, were gathered together at Montreal to attend the funeral which had been appointed to take place on Easter Monday, the 13th April, 1868, being the anniversary, as we have elsewhere said, of his forty-third birth day. The public jour-nals of the province have very accurately described the incidents and particulars of that impressive pageant. Our space will not permit us to add to their narratives, but we cannot deny ourselves the gratification of including in our cursory work the eloquent and impressive sermon, as it is reported in the *Montreal Herald*, which was delivered on the occasion, in St. Patrick's Church, by the Rev. Mr. O'Farrell, who, as the personal friend as well as the spiritual counsellor of the deceased, had much right to speak with earnestness of his character, as well as of the opinions and princi-ples by which it had been regulated and controlled.

THE FUNERAL SERMON.

The Rev. Mr. O'FARRELL then ascended the pulpit and gave out the text :—

" How is the mighty man fallen, that saved the people of Israel."—I Machabees, ix. 21.

He said : Such, dearly beloved, was the cry of sorrow that burst from the hearts of the Jewish people, that re-echoed along the plains and amongst the hills of Judæa, when the doleful news was brought, that Judas Machabeus, their skilful captain, their heroic leader, had fallen at last upon the field of battle, fighting in the cause of his country's freedom. "And all the people of Israel bewailed with great lamentation, and they mourned for him many days, and said : 'How is the mighty man fallen, that saved the people of Israel.'" May we not, ought we not, to give utterance to a similar outburst of grief on this most lamentable occasion which has united us all here to-day ? And, in presence of these poor relics of mortality, which remind us so powerfully of one who, by his brilliant genius, his soul-stirring eloquence, his far-seeing wisdom, contributed so much to the safety and renown of this country, shall we not say, as did the Jews of old : " How is the mighty man fallen, that saved the people ?" He did not, it is true, perish on the field of battle, amidst the clang of arms and tumult of the conflict ; but he died in as noble a field. Although struck down by the foulest murder that ever darkened our annals, he died as certainly for the land of his adoption, and with a soul as unflinching and a heart as brave as ever beat in a soldier's breast, and "therefore the people of this land have bewailed him with great lamentations, "and they sorrow for him, and shall not cease to mourn him for many days." When the illustrious French soldier, Latour d'Auvergne, the first grenadier of France, as he was simply, yet honorably, styled, died in the service of his country, his name was still retained on the muster roll of his regiment, and, when called out by the commanding officer on service days, as if he were still present, the oldest soldier would step out of the ranks, and, amid the solemn silence of his comrades, reply in these touching words: "Died on the field of honor." And so, my brethren, when the muster roll of the great men of Canada shall be read out to future generations, to the name of Thomas D'Arcy McGee shall be added, as his best and most suitable epitaph, that he "died on the field of honor." In the midst of the general grief, I have been requested to give utterance, before this magnificent assembly of the rulers and statesmen and leaders of our country, to the feelings that have stirred to the very centre the heart of the nation, and, although I well know that my words, feeble and languid, can serve but as a very imperfect echo to the emotions with which your hearts are throbbing, still I have willingly accepted the invitation, because I admired and esteemed in the deceased the *Scholar*, whose mind was stored and enriched with the most varied information ; the *Patriot*, who loved his country, his native as well as his adopted one, with the truest and deepest affection ; the *Statesman*, whose mighty intellect soared above all merely local interests, and comprehended in his far-reaching glance the necessities and advantages of the entire Empire ; but, more than all, as a minister of God, I loved and admirer the humble *Christian*, who devoted his talents to the noblest causes, whose faith in the doctrines of the Catholic Church shone out all the brighter and purer after the storms by which it had been tested, and towards the close of his life he especially showed the firmest hope and the most touching confidence in the merits and mercies of his crucified master. To dilate on these different phases of his character at any great length would detain us beyond reasonable limits. I shall, therefore, refer to each of them in a brief, simple manner. Others, with more eloquent voices, but not with a more loving heart, shall develope them elsewhere. No one amongst you is ignorant of the extraordinary talents and wonderful abilities that distinguished the deceased. His mind was one of the richest and most deeply stored with the wisdom of past ages that I have ever been acquainted with, not the mere knowledge of date and facts, and all the dry bones of history, but with the living spirit which enabled him to penetrate into the causes and calculate the consequences of the mighty revolutions of the past, and weigh them with the precision of a master. And when his graceful imagination turned to the cultivation of the masses, a perennial well spring of the sweetest poetry bubbled up from his heart. But what shall I say of that marvellous gift of eloquence which used to entrance the thousands that so often assembled to drink in those limpid streams that flowed so deliciously, so enchantingly from his lips. Our ears are yet ravished with the silvery tones of that magnificent voice, that stirred every fibre of our hearts like the rising and the swelling of the Œolian harp. Alas ! that voice is now stilled for ever, those sweet accents shall never more charm our souls; the skilful performer, who once played upon our very heart strings, and, drew from them such delicious feelings, has been stricken down in the prime of his manhood, by a most dastardly blow ; and as when a strain of glorious music has suddenly ceased, our souls feel an aching void, a painful longing to catch once more those harmonious sounds :—

> " Sweet voice of comfort! 't was like the stealing
> " Of summer wind through some wreathed shell;
> " Each secret winding, each inmost feeling,
> " Of all my soul, echoed to its spell.
> " 'T was whispered balm, 't was sunshine spoken.
> " I'd live through years of grief and pain,
> " To have my long sleep of sorrow broken
> " By such benign blessed sounds again."

2. But why dwell longer on what all of you know even better than I do, for you have been oftener witnesses to the wonderful versatility of his mind, which could pass with such ease from grave to gay, and from the abstrusest problems of social science, to the highest scenes of poetical fancy? And after all, if Mr. McGee were only a man of talent, if his abililities had been of no use to his country, if he were not a patriot as well as a scholar, I should not stand here to-day to praise his memory, even though his genius had been a hundred fold greater than it was. Love of country, my brethren, is no selfish feeling, no narrow confining of the affections of the heart, it is a feeling implanted by God himself in the hearts of even the most untutored, that makes us love the land which gave us birth, no matter how poor or how oppressed, better than the proudest or most glorious of the nations of the earth. It was this feeling which animated the Royal Prophet when he exclaimed, "If I forget thee, O Jerusalem, may my right hand be forgotten, may my tongue cleave to my jaws, if I do not remember thee, if I make not Jerusalem the beginning of my joy." It was this feeling which made our blessed Lord shed tears of sorrow over his ungrateful Jerusalem, and so well was his love of country known to the Jews, that when they wished to obtain from him a miracle in favor of the centurion, they considered that no argument would be more efficacious than to remind the Saviour that this stranger loved their nation. If, then, Mr. McGee had proved recreant to his native land, no words of mine should ever sound in his praise, and I should allow him to remain, as a great writer said of him whose soul was dead to this generous feeling, "unwept, unhonored and unsung." Never was a fouler calumny uttered than that the deceased was a traitor to Ireland. There was scarcely a pulse of his heart that did not beat for her, scarcely a poem or a song, or more extensive work from his pen, that had not Ireland for his theme. There was scarcely a legend of the old land unknown to him, scarcely a monument or a ruin in it which was not celebrated by him either in verse or prose, not an association formed for the cultivation of her literature in which he had not some share, not a national movement for her prosperity which was not encouraged by him. I never knew a man who thought more constantly, or more affectionately of Ireland. She was the inspirer of his verse— the theme of his prose. He loved her with a passionate ardor, like that of a lover for his mistress. He loved everything about Ireland, except the shortcomings of her people. From his early boyhood his pen was devoted to her service. His warm imagination and passionate heart took fire at what he deemed her unbearable wrongs, and he threw himself into a movement which we all know was foolish and most ill timed. He loved Ireland then, not wisely but too well. And when in after years he condemned his youthful impetuosity, did he then cease to love his country? Read over the passionate outpourings of his heart in verse, read over the list of his larger writings, and you will find that he has scarcely another theme. Look at his "Irish Settlers in America," the "Attempt to establish the Reformation in Ireland," the "Life of Dr. Maginn," and greatest of all his "History of Ireland," which is confessedly the best which has been written, and more wonderful has been written upon a foreign soil, with such

scanty material as he could here procure. How then could some of our people come to be convinced that he had renounced and vilified his native land? Ah! my brethren, the power of calumny is fearful for a time. Every stray word, every unguarded expression that fell from his lips, was taken hold of by his enemies, and paraded, and repeated again and again until it sank into many persons' hearts, and became so deeply rooted there, that nothing would eradicate it. Advantage, too, was taken of the honest, outspoken indignation with which he reprobated the nefarious attempts of a miserable, disgraceful conspiracy to enter into this peaceable land, and to avenge the wrongs of Ireland upon Canada, the happy homes of your children. Yes, if he was guilty of a crime against Ireland because he denounced the abominable plots of men who only bring shame and disgrace upon her, then I too am guilty of the same crime, for I denounce to-day, as vehemently as he could do, such vile, unprincipled means; and if it be proved that his death was the result of his enmity to those secret societies, then I call upon every honest man to stamp out with horror, every vestige of them from amongst us. There must be no sympathy for such a dastardly crime, the man or woman who could feel any joy at such a diabolical deed, would be as horrible to my soul as the assassin himself. (There was here an involuntary movement of applause, quickly checked by the preacher, who reminded the audience that it was the house of God.) Mr. McGee, then, was not false to his own land, although he tried to serve to the utmost of his power his adopted one. I shall quote for you a sentence from his own speech on last St. Patrick's Day in Ottawa, when alluding to this charge against him: "If I have avoided for two or three years much speaking in public on the subject of Ireland, even in a literary or historical sense, I do not admit that I can be fairly charged in consequence with being either a sordid or a cold hearted Irishman. I utterly deny, because I could not stand still and see our peaceful, unoffending Canada invaded and deluged in blood, in the abused and unauthorized name of Ireland, that therefore I was a bad Irishman. I utterly deny the audacious charge, and I say that my mental labors will prove, such as they are, that I know Ireland as well, in her strength and in weakness, and love her as dearly as those who, in ignorance of my Canadian position, in ignorance of my obligations to my adopted country, not to speak of my solemn oath of office, have made this cruelly false charge against me." After which he alluded to the fact that he had brought the wrongs of Ireland before the chief authorities in England, and he adds, "that he believed he was doing-Ireland a good turn in the proper quarter." I deem it unnecessary to dwell longer upon a point which, to my mind, is of the clearest evidence, nor should I have treated it at all at such length, if all the hatred which has been excited against the deceased, and which, I fear, has culminated in his death, so awful and so shocking, had not sprung from such unfounded, such base calumnious charges, which were blindly believed in by some of my countrymen. But it is true that the heart of the deceased was large enough to admit of other affections. Beside the love of Ireland, there grew up in it another love, almost as strong and enduring—the love of Canada, and under the influence of that new feeling his mind took a wider compass, his views became more enlarged and liberal, his glance became more far reaching, and he rose from being the patriot of one country, to be the statesman that embraced the entire empire in his views. Others shall tell you what he did to build up a public spirit in this country—what labors he underwent to infuse a great national feeling into all inhabitants—how he strove earnestly to unite all nationalities and creeds together, and to diffuse a common spirit of charity, good feeling and brotherly love among all the children of the soil. When the necessity made itself felt that all parts of this vast region should become linked more closely together,.

whose voice was more frequently raised to cement and consolidate all the parts
of this new Dominion? It is a significant, although a melancholy fact, that the last
speech which his eloquent lips uttered, was in defence of the Union which would
make this country a great and prosperous nation, and thus his parting legacy, I
may say his dying words, were an exhortation to concord and peace, securing to
him for ever in the gratitude of his countrymen, the title which he desired most
during his life, that of "peacemaker." Torn from amongst us while yet so young,
scarcely forty-three years old, his mind had not yet attained its full development,
and marvellous as have been the proofs of his genius, we shall never know to what
a height he might yet have soared, if Providence had spared him to us for a longer
time. With the new view of things which he had acquired during his late illness,
and the renewed determination to apply himself still more closely to his duties,
he might have become the greatest statesman of this new world, and worthy to
be placed in comparison with the most illustrious names in the annals of Europe.
Yet, my brethren, why should I, a minister of God, dwell upon such merely human
qualities? Here, in the presence of the Most High, and with that poor corpse lying
cold and motionless before us, must we not be inevitably reminded of the vanity of
all earthly creatures, and of the words of Jesus Christ, "What doth it profit a man
if he gain the whole world and lose his own soul, and what will a man give in exchange for his soul." T. D. McGee is now before a tribunal where earthly renown is
counted for very little, and where the Judge will not inquire whether he was a good
poet, or an eloquent orator, or a clever statesman, but whether he was a sincere and
humble Christian, and employed well the gifts which he had received from above.
As far as human knowledge can go, I believe the deceased did earnestly strive to
prepare himself for the great account which we must all one day render to Him
who is the Judge of the living and the dead. He had his faults, every one knows
—let those who are without them cast the first stone at him. In his early days,
when soured and disappointed with the defeat and failure of his cherished plans,
he seemed for a while to be shaken in his love for the Church, which would not
approve of revolutionary schemes, but when the mists of passion cleared away
from his soul, the light of religion shone out all the brighter upon him. Nor was
his faith a mere speculative belief in the doctrines of the Catholic Church. He
was also an humble, and, despite of human frailty, a sincere observer of her teachings. One thing was very remarkable in his character. It was the simple, unaffected way in which he was ever ready to aid in any cause of benevolence. I
remember when I once invited him to give a lecture for some object that was
dear to me, he chose for his theme, "Heroic Charity," and it struck me then, as
it does now, that he himself might be considered as exemplifying the subject in
his own person. But his religious feelings became more intense and sincere during the long illness to which Providence was pleased to subject him. During the
lonely hours of his convalescence, his mind pondered deeply on the great truths
of religion, and he himself often spoke of the beneficial effects upon his soul of
those consoling mysteries. The result of these meditations might be seen in the
increased fervor with which he prepared to receive the Sacraments which Christ
instituted to satisfy the wants of the soul, and in the public fulfilment in this
Church, on the day before he departed from Montreal, of those duties which are
imposed upon Catholics at Easter time. This change might also be seen in the
resolution which he kept so inviolably until the day of his death, to abstain from
those social excesses which would mar so considerably the effect of his talents.
Let those who are tempted as he was, appreciate the amount of self-sacrifice
which such a resolution involved. Finally, this change might be seen in the earnest tones of the few writings or speeches which were lately prepared by him, but

in none, perhaps, better than in the very affecting lines which he composed as a song of requiem to a departed friend, beside whose coffin he stood in those very aisles only one short month ago. I cannot conclude better than by quoting some of those lines, as the portrait which he painted of his friend will now serve to describe himself.

> " His Faith was as the tested gold,
> " His Hope assured, not over-bold,
> " His Charities past count untold,
>   *Miserere Domine.*
>
> " Well may they grieve, who laid him there,
> " Where shall they find his equal ? Where ?
> " Nought can avail him now but prayer.
>   *Miserere Domine.*"

With this mournful dirge I commend his memory to your care. May his lessons never be lost upon us. May his death on behalf of his country serve to give strength to our hearts to do or die, if necessary in her cause; and as we are all united here to-day around the body of Thomas D'Arcy McGee, may we become more and more united in brotherly feeling and holy charity, all animated with his spirit, all laboring for the same great ends, and then from those ashes, in this holy Easter time, a new country shall spring, and with his blood shall be watered and fostered the young tree of our national greatness. And when we shall have thus served our country here below, may we all pass to the better country above, to bless and praise our God for ever. AMEN.

The affecting service at St. Patrick's was supplemented by a still more imposing ceremonial at the Roman Catholic Parish Church, where the Queen's subjects of French origin are accustomed to worship ; eight thousand persons, it was conjectured, stood within the walls of that spacious building when the coffin, borne by friends, and followed by mourners, was carried to its allotted place in the centre of the central aisle. The continuous roll of muffled music caught by successive bands and transmitted from street to street and square to square, seemed to grow in volume and intensity as the procession arrived within the Place d'Armes, and drew near to the entrance of the Church. Then, as the cries of inferior animals in the desert are said to subside when the lion roars, so all instruments of lesser note, were hushed, as with throbbing breath the great organ of Notre Dame took up the burden of their grief, and in strains of unapproachable pathos and emotion gave with thrilling effect, the Dead March in Saul. White robed priests and minute chorister boys, in number without number, moved with noiseless celerity to their stalls. All was still, for unusual interest was manifested as the Right Reverend Monseigneur Bourget, the Roman Catholic Bishop of Montreal, with two attendant priests advanced to the front of the Altar, while the former with visible emotion, which age, recent illness, and present suffering, were well calculated to increase, delivered a very solemn and touching address, a portion of which we very imperfectly translate. After speaking of the heinousness of the crime, the Venerable Bishop added:

" By this demonstration you render homage to a citizen, who, it may be, having committed faults knew how to atone for them nobly, and it was for this atonement he was doomed to die by the hand of an assassin. He went home thinking that he was unlocking the door of his earthly house, and he found himself on the threshold of 'the house not made with hands,' where, let us hope, the God of mercy was waiting to receive him. In the midst of these sad surroundings this grand demonstration teaches us that while an individual may be assassinated, a people cannot be slain. Murderers will see that a nation has only one heart and one soul, and that both are set against them. Where all are resolved to support the cause of order and society no fear need be entertained for the machinations of assassins."

The solemn service ended, the procession of mourners was again formed. Following the car, whereon the coffin was placed for the last time, they silently ascended the slope of what formerly was called "Mont Royal" to the quiet cemetery where D'Arcy McGee's last resting place had already been prepared. Public buildings were passed, and thronged thoroughfares left behind, but along the country roads flag staffs had been improvised, and banners at half mast suspended; for private individuals vied with public bodies in doing honor to one who had earnestly striven to confer benefits on all. The picturesque burial place was at length reached. In traversing its quiet pathways one could not fail to note the manner in which faith and love, memory and hope, had striven to adorn it. A local newspaper described the scene as "a forest of marble." Truly the emblems of mortality and of redemption were there, the obelisk and the cross, one pointing to the skies and the other telling of the way there. Could the slumberer of immortality have spoken to us from his shroud, he might then with impassioned eloquence have read "sermons in stones" as truly as he had elsewhere taught that there was "good in every thing."